UP THE RED ~~

ABOUT THE AUTHOR

Margot Bosonnet has penned hundreds of comic and serious poems for many years while raising her family. She is the author of *Skyscraper Ted and Other Zany Verse* (Wolfhound 1994) and lives in Co. Dublin.

ABOUT THE ILLUSTRATOR

Sarah Cunningham is an illustrator and author of *Topsy-Turvy Tales* (Children's Poolbeg 1995). She lives and works in Dublin.

By the same author

Skyscraper Ted and Other Zany Verse
(Wolfhound Press, 1994)

UP THE RED BELLY

Margot Bosonnet

Illustrated by Sarah Cunningham

WOLFHOUND PRESS

First published 1996 by
WOLFHOUND PRESS Ltd
68 Mountjoy Square
Dublin 1

Wolfhound Press receives financial assistance from the Arts Council/
An Chomhairle Ealaíon, Dublin.

British Library Cataloguing in Publication Data
A catalogue record for this book is available from the British Library.

ISBN 0 86327 530 3

Cover illustration: Sara Cunningham
Cover design: Joe Gervin
Typesetting: Wolfhound Press
Printed in the UK by Cox & Wyman, Reading, Berkshire.

Contents

To Malahide Writer's Workshop, especially Barbara, who brought me along, and Mary, Clare and Karina who started it all and got me writing.

Up The Red Belly

Joan always maintained that the trouble they got into that summer was entirely due to the arrival of Mackey.

Jonathan disagreed – they were quite able to make their own trouble long before him, thank you very much!

Felicity called it coincidence, which was rather nice of her considering she suffered more than anyone else.

But even Felicity had to agree that things had a way of going badly wrong whenever Mackey was around ...

Chapter 1
News for the gang

'Jonathan.'
 'Jonathan!'
 'Jon-a-than!'
 Jonathan belted down the lane, away from the calling voice. At the bottom he turned, where the lane swung round to form a wide avenue behind the houses – and a buffer zone between the back gardens and Conker Woods. Halfway down he turned again, plunging straight in through the trees. He ran and ran until he came to a clearing with a single enormous tree in the middle. This he rapidly climbed, up and up, to a point where the massive trunk divided into a spread of thick branches.
 Jonathan disappeared.

☆☆☆

Felicity was fed up. As a matter of fact, she was more than fed up: she was hopping mad. He'd done it again. As she hurried down the lane she wished, not for the first time, that she was a boy. They got away with murder. It just wasn't fair.
 At the bottom of the lane she headed straight into the woods and turned left, following a small path behind some houses whose gardens ran straight

9

down to the woods. She left the path and battled her way through a mixture of trees and bushes until she came to a place where the thick undergrowth looked completely impenetrable. Dropping down onto her tummy, she wriggled in under a tangle of bushes for a few feet, until her head emerged into the Tunnel.

It was one of their hidey-holes – formed by the arch of a huge old hedge against a wall, both long since overgrown with brambles and weeds until no one knew they were there any more – except the gang. They had found it by accident. It was long and narrow, and you had to sit or lie down because the hedging was so low overhead.

Felicity elbowed her way completely in.

'You're late,' said Joan, yawning lazily. She was stretched out on her back reading a comic.

'I know.' Felicity pulled herself alongside on her tummy. 'I had to do Jonathan's jobs as well as my own. Mum called him for ages and he wouldn't answer, so she nabbed me just as I was coming out and made me do them .... It's not fair ... I know he's hiding up the Red Belly – as usual.'

Joan looked disapproving.

Felicity glared at her friend, having had sufficient lack of sympathy for one morning. 'Don't look at me like that, Joan O'Brien – just because you have a crush on Jonathan!'

Joan went very red. 'I have not.'

'Well, why do you always stand up for him lately?'

Joan looked uncomfortable, but defensive. She tossed her short dark hair back. 'It's just ... I think you don't appreciate him.'

'Appreciate him! Why should I appreciate him, when he sneaks off every time it's his turn to do something?'

'He probably didn't hear your Mum calling,' said Joan. 'He might be down in Muggins's house. Anyway, if I had a brother like Jonathan I wouldn't mind doing things for him. I think you're lucky – you don't know what it's like to be an only child.'

Felicity looked at her friend without a shred of sympathy. Joan was spoilt rotten by her granny who lived with them. She was never asked to do anything around the house anyway, so how could she know? 'Well, you're welcome to him,' said Felicity with feeling.

Felicity and Jonathan were twins. No one could ever believe it, which was half the trouble. Jonathan was tall, blond and handsome, with skin that had an almost permanent tan. People tended to admire him – though, in fairness, he didn't seek such admiration – just took it for granted as a normal fact of life. He could have a condescending manner towards girls, but he liked Orla, who was almost a year older, and had a grudging respect for Joan as she could beat him at running over most distances.

Felicity, on the other hand, was small for her age, with long brown hair and freckles. She hated her freckles. 'Sunkisses', her mother called them, which didn't help a bit. But most of all she hated being small because she couldn't climb the Red Belly. She was the only one of the gang who couldn't, although she was a very good climber apart from that. But her arms simply wouldn't stretch to the difficult handholds on the Red Belly's enormous trunk. It was a very sore point.

Joan and Felicity lay in the Tunnel without speaking. Felicity was hurt by her friend's attitude, and Joan was insulted by Felicity's.

They might have stayed like that for the rest of the morning if it wasn't for the arrival of Orla, who slid noisily into the Tunnel and squeezed herself in between them.

'Hear ye! Hear ye! I bring tidings of great joy ... Hey, what's up?' Orla looked from one to the other, suddenly sensing the mood.

'Nothing,' said Felicity quickly. Orla was the eldest of six children and was always having to mind the little ones. She did this with such unfailing good cheer that Felicity was ashamed to admit she had been complaining about a few chores.

'What tidings?' asked Joan, perking up.

'I can't tell, I promised Muggins. We've to tell everyone together – meeting now at the Captain's Table.'

'Can't we hold the meeting here?'

'It's too squashy. Besides, it's a lovely morning. So come on!'

They squeezed their way back out of the Tunnel and stood up, brushing the earth off their clothes.

'Where's Jonathan?' asked Felicity.

'He's up the Red Belly,' said Orla. 'He'll be down in a minute.'

Felicity shot a triumphant look at Joan.

☆☆☆

Muggins and Jonathan were already waiting by the Captain's Table, which was a big fallen tree on the edge of a clearing. The Red Belly was meant to be their headquarters, but since Felicity couldn't climb it, they had to hold their meetings here instead. The roots of the tree spiralled into the air like a wheel, and there were lots of branches sticking out along the trunk. The branches were fun to sit on as you could bounce them up and down, and there was plenty of room for everyone.

'I want to tell first,' said Muggins when they were all seated. He was nearly bursting with excitement.

Orla laughed at her brother. 'Oh, go on then.'

'Somebody's bought Dara's house at last! They're moving in next Saturday.'

'Who told you?' asked Felicity in surprise.

'My Mum. She met Dara's granny yesterday.'

'Any kids?'

'One. A boy. And guess what? He's our age too!' Muggins looked pleased at having come out with the most important piece of information.

'Great, great, great!' whooped Jonathan, clapping his hands. They had been so afraid that Dara's house would go to somebody with no children at all.

Dara was one of the Red Belly gang – or had been until late last year. Then his father, who was a teacher, got this overwhelming urge to go and help people in the Third World. He had taken the whole family to Zambia, and Dara was sorely missed.

'And that's not all,' added Orla. 'He comes from a pub in the city.'

There was an awed silence all round as the gang savoured this piece of news.

'You mean he actually lives in a pub?' Jonathan whistled softly.

'Well, his Dad owns one.'

Muggins broke in again. 'My Mum says he's a poor deprived child who probably never saw a green field in his life.'

'That's all we want.' Joan grimaced in disgust. 'Someone who can't even climb a tree.'

'We can teach him,' said Jonathan quickly. 'It's not his fault if he's never done things like that – stuck in a pub all his life ... I wonder if he'll be coming to school with us?'

'Of course he will,' said Muggins.

'Maybe he'll stay at his own school until the summer holidays.'

'They mightn't want to move him at all,' said Orla. 'He could still travel in and out to the city.'

Jonathan's face fell. 'That'd be awful. We'd never get to know him then.'

'Maybe he won't want to know us,' Felicity pointed out.

'How do we know that somebody new in the gang won't spoil things anyway?' asked Joan.

They were all silent for a moment, considering this point.

Orla firmly put an end to their doubts. 'Well ... I think it's great to have somebody new coming, and it's up to us to make friends.'

✩✩✩

The gang spent the rest of the morning playing their favourite game – tree-chasing. The woods contained the most marvellous collection of climbing trees imaginable. Some were very old and gnarled, and some were straight and tall. There were fallen trees which formed bridges and ramps in the most unexpected places, turning the whole woods into an aerial playground.

Tree-chasing was their particular speciality. The only rule of the game was that no one could touch the ground. You could climb any tree as high as you liked, or swing from tree to tree to avoid being caught, but once you put a foot on the ground you were out. By unspoken agreement they never said anything about these chasing games to their parents – who would, no doubt, have considered them too dangerous. There was no point in looking for trouble.

But the Red Belly was their pride and joy.

It was the tallest tree in the woods, very very old, and it stood in a clearing of its own, some distance away from the Captain's Table. It got its name from a huge daub of red paint on the trunk, which had been there as long as any of the gang could remember.

The Red Belly had no branches at all near the ground, which made it extremely difficult to climb. It took the agility of a monkey and the skill of a mountaineer to find the cracks and bumps that served as precarious finger and toe holds up the trunk. The first big overhanging branch seemed impossibly far away, but once this was reached, the rest of the tree was easy work for any competent climber.

Halfway up, the tree split into a spread of thick branches. In this giant fork was a hollow which could hold several people without their being seen from the ground. There was plenty of room, too, for sitting on the branches around the fork. This was the gang's headquarters; they called it the Crow's Nest. Here, too, were nooks and crannies where they hid things – letters, postcards, a logbook, odd treasures, and sunflower seeds and raisins for survival rations.

From the very top of the Red Belly, which was level with the church spire, you could see just about everywhere: the city way off on the horizon, the sea far away to the left. You could see into the back gardens on Conker Road – especially the middle ones, with the lane behind, where the gang lived. Not everybody had a lane – the houses at the top and bottom of the road had gardens that ran right down to the woods. No one knew why, it was just the way they were built.

The Red Belly was a brilliant tree, and they planned to hold all their gang meetings up in the Crow's Nest as soon as Felicity was able to reach it.

This, then, was the territory that awaited the new arrival.

CHAPTER 2
THE ARRIVAL

On saturday morning, Felicity volunteered to do lookout.

None of them wanted to stand out on the front road, making it obvious that they were waiting for the newcomers. So Felicity ran up the lane every few minutes to check if they had arrived, while the rest of the gang waited in the woods. She ran up and down so many times that finally Mrs Finnerty, who lived in the house across the lane from Felicity's, shouted at her as she ran past, 'Just a minute. Just a minute. Just a minute now, young lady!'

Felicity stopped. Mrs Finnerty was out in the garden cutting her hedge. Her own children were all grown up and gone away, and she was forever giving out. She glared at Felicity from the top of the step-ladder. 'What do you think you are doing?' she demanded.

'Just going up the lane, Mrs Finnerty.'

'Up, down, up, down, up, down. Are you going to run up and down all morning?'

'No, Mrs Finnerty.'

'And you were playing ball in the lane again last night,' she accused.

Felicity and Joan had been playing two-balls against Felicity's gable wall after tea. 'We weren't playing up against your wall, Mrs Finnerty.'

'No, but I still hear the noise, don't I? Thud, thud, thud! When my children were your age they were in bed by six o'clock.'

'That's why they all left home,' muttered Felicity.

'What's that?'

'Can I go now, Mrs Finnerty?'

Mrs Finnerty waved her away with a flick of the wrist, and Felicity ran to the top of the lane.

There was a car parked outside Dara's house, and a removal van. Some men were busy unlatching the back of the van. Felicity turned and crept back down the lane again, bending double as she passed by Finnerty's in the hope that Mrs Finnerty wouldn't see her.

The rest of the gang were sitting at the Captain's Table.

'Quick! Quick! Come quick – they've arrived!'

They took to their heels out of the woods and raced full speed up the lane, leaving Mrs Finnerty purple with fury, shaking her fist and shouting after them, 'I'll tell your mothers! I'll tell your mothers!'

They sat on a wall across the road from Dara's house, where they could see what was going on. A big wardrobe was being carried in. They watched with interest as the removal men manoeuvred it expertly through the door and up the stairs.

'I'd like to be a removal man when I grow up,' declared Muggins.

'Well, I wouldn't,' said Felicity, giggling. 'I'd be all muscles.'

'I wonder where the new people are?'

'Busy putting all the things away, I suppose.'

Jonathan was getting impatient. 'I hope we don't have to wait half the morning to see them – should we go over?'

'No, we'd hardly be welcome just yet,' Orla warned.

They hung around, watching, until it didn't seem possible that any more stuff could appear out of the van.

'Look!' said Jonathan. 'There he is.'

A boy came wandering out into the front garden. He didn't see them at first.

'He's awfully small,' said Jonathan. 'I thought you said he was our age?'

'He is too,' asserted Muggins. 'It's probably a lack of clean air that's stopped him growing properly. People in cities grow up sort of poisoned – I read that somewhere.'

They eyed the new arrival with interest. Having spotted his audience, he sat on the front pillar, put his fingers to his lips, and emitted a piercing whistle.

They all jumped.

'He does that even better than Jonathan,' said Felicity admiringly.

'Well, nearly,' said Joan, with a quick glance at Jonathan to see if he was offended. But Jonathan was grinning. He put his fingers to his mouth and whistled back.

First contact over he led the way across the road, and they stood in line by the edge of the pavement.

'Hi, I'm Jonathan Kelly – I live in the house beside the lane.'

There was a long pause. The new boy was clearly sizing them up before deciding to speak. Jonathan became embarrassed at the silence.

'What's your name?' he asked at last.

'Ignatius McCarthy.' The rich city accent caught them by surprise. 'And if you call me Iggy, I'll thump you!'

'We'll call you whatever you want,' said Jonathan primly, taken aback at the show of aggression. 'Why don't you like Iggy?'

'It's poncy, that's why!' – and he looked so fierce that they all laughed, suddenly breaking the ice.

'OK, what'll we call you then?'

'My friends call me Mackey.'

'Right. Mackey it is then.'

He stepped aside to introduce the others.

'This is Orla Duggan and this is Joan O'Brien.' The girls nodded hello. 'And this is Michael Duggan, Orla's brother. He's called Muggins for short ... and this is my sister Felicity.'

'That's a queer name,' said Mackey. 'Worse than mine. Why did your Ma call you something like that?'

Felicity shrugged. She was used to people remarking on her name.

'My Mum says it's to make up for having a name like Kelly.'

'What's wrong with Kelly?'

'I don't know. I don't think she likes it very much.'

'They're twins,' said Orla.

'Who?'

'Felicity and Jonathan.'

'You're kidding.' Mackey looked at them in disbelief.

'We're non-identical,' said Jonathan loftily.

'I can see that.'

Felicity kicked at the pavement. She didn't like this conversation.

'You two are more like the twins,' observed Mackey, looking at Orla and Muggins, who both had dark red hair.

'Well, we're not,' said Orla decisively.

'Did you really live in a pub?' Muggins couldn't wait any longer to get the question in.

'Yeah. Well, not in the pub – over it.'

'Is the pub sold then?' asked Jonathan.

'Not at all. My Da is still there. He'll come out here on days off.'

'Why did you leave it, so?'

Mackey grinned. 'My Ma said I was getting too bloody streetwise.'

The gang looked at one another, not really sure what he meant, but unwilling to let their side down by asking.

'Well,' said Jonathan at last, 'you'll really like it here. There's a brilliant wood at the back of the house – we hang out there a lot.'

'Like all the time.'

'And guess what we do ... ?' Suddenly they were all talking together, each trying to get a word in edgewise in their impatience to let Mackey know the treats that were in store for him.

'... And we understand,' butted in Muggins at one point, 'that you'll take a bit of getting used to the trees, on account of never having seen a green field before.'

Mackey looked at Muggins incredulously. 'What's he talking about?'

Jonathan rescued the situation quickly. 'Don't mind him – he's bats.'

Poor Muggins looked so offended that they all laughed.

'We'll show you our trees,' said Orla. 'The very best ones for climbing.'

'And the Red Belly, and the Captain's Table, and the Tunnel.'

'And you'll be climbing really well in no time at all,' said Jonathan. 'Just wait and see. We'll all help you.'

Mackey grinned, but said nothing.

'Do you want to come round to the woods now?' asked Jonathan hopefully.

'Can't ... I've to go back in and help my Ma put everything away. She said I was to help today.'

'Well, tomorrow then?'

'OK.'

'Right, we'll call for you in the morning.'

'Hey, I have to go,' said Mackey suddenly. 'My Ma's banging on the window at me ... see you.'

With a bound, he jumped down from the pillar and disappeared into the house.

CHAPTER 3
IN THE WOODS

At ten o'clock next morning they trooped up Mackey's back garden and knocked on the door.

Mrs McCarthy answered it. She was very pretty, small and dark like Mackey, but she seemed a little anxious, puffing away on a cigarette all the time they were introducing themselves.

'Can we help you at all, Mrs McCarthy?' asked Felicity, thinking that maybe she was overworked.

'I could do with a drill. Does your Da have one?'

'No, but my Mum has. She does all that sort of thing in our house.'

'That's great. I could do with some information too.'

'I'll go and tell my Mum.' Felicity raced back home and sought out her mother, who was up in the spare bedroom, busy at her computer. Mrs Kelly had gone back to work recently. She only did two mornings a week for the moment, but had to study a lot at home to catch up on her skills. That was why the housework business had reached crisis proportions this summer. She needed Jonathan and Felicity to do more jobs than usual to give her time to work at the computer.

Felicity told her mother about Mrs McCarthy.

'Yes,' said Mrs Kelly, 'I was going to pop in this morning anyway – I was just giving them a bit of time to settle. I'd hate anyone to walk in on me before things were organised.'

Felicity ran back to tell Mrs McCarthy that her mother was coming. She found the gang admiring a big black Labrador who was sunning himself on the path.

'This is Boozer,' introduced Mackey. 'He's old. He used to be our guard dog. But my Ma says he deserves a better place than a city pub to spend his retirement. He likes it here already, don't you Boozer?' He threw his arms around Boozer's neck and kissed him.

Boozer woke up and licked Mackey's face, then settled down to sleep again as if to say 'Now leave me alone.'

☆☆☆

So Mackey's indoctrination into the woods began.

They showed him all the best trees, and explained at great length the merits of each one. They pointed out the footholds and handholds, and where the most difficult bits were.

Mackey took it all in without saying much. Hands stuck in his pockets, he watched as the rest of the gang, under Jonathan's direction, gave him a demonstration of tree-climbing.

Then they introduced him to the Tunnel, the various paths they used through the woods, and the big field at the back. When they came to the Captain's Table they all sat down for a rest.

Mackey, having settled into a comfortable position among the branches, reached into his jacket pocket and took out half a cigarette. A good rummage in his other pocket produced a small book of matches. He lit up and inhaled deeply. Then, carefully, he pursed his lips and blew a perfect smoke ring into the air.

Jonathan whistled softly. 'Wow! How about that!'

They all stared at Mackey, impressed.

'Anyone want a fag?' Mackey dipped into his pocket again and brought out a generous handful of cigarette butts. He passed them around.

Jonathan took the book of matches and gave everyone a light.

Orla burned her fingers trying to light a butt that was too short and dropped it quickly. Mackey gave her another one, rooting through his store to pick out the longest one he had.

Felicity took tiny careful puffs, holding the smoke in her mouth until she could decently get rid of it, trying not to inhale any.

Joan, however, inhaled deeply and started to cough and choke. Running to the nearest bush, she got sick.

Mackey roared with laughter.

'Hey – she's never smoked before.'

'I have so,' said Joan furiously, between bouts of coughing – even though she hadn't. She would not give Mackey the satisfaction of admitting it.

Muggins was looking a bit sick too, and giving little half-coughs, but he managed to keep going.

Orla was blowing into her butt instead of inhaling – a trick Jonathan had shown her once, so it looked like she was smoking.

Mackey leaned back and blew another smoke ring, a huge one this time – then another; then a whole chain of little rings.

'How did you learn to do that?'

'Fella in the pub taught me. It's dead easy. I'll show you.' Mackey demonstrated slowly and patiently, but try as they might, the others couldn't produce a single smoke ring between them.

Mackey was starting on his third cigarette butt by the time the rest of the gang had finished their first. As no one else wanted any more, they headed off in the direction of the Red Belly. They had deliberately left it until last.

Mackey blew more smoke rings as they walked along, showing off quite shamelessly.

When they reached the Red Belly, Jonathan explained all about it, pointing out the features that made it such a great tree.

'The bottom bit is hard to climb – Felicity can't manage it yet.'

'But I'm going to, this summer,' said Felicity, with more confidence than she actually felt.

Mackey looked up at the tree. 'Why don't you knock a few nails in it?' he asked. 'Or hang a rope from a branch?'

Jonathan looked horrified. 'That's cheating. Either you can climb, or you can't. But,' he added hastily, 'it doesn't matter if you can't climb it for a while. We'll start you on some of the easier trees first ... let you work your way up to the harder ones.'

Mackey stamped out his fag-end and carefully sized up the tree. Then, before any of them could so much as blink an eye, he was scaling the trunk, hands and knees flying straight up without a pause to the first branch. He stopped for a moment to grin down at them, then continued on, up to the Crow's Nest. He disappeared out of sight.

'What's here? Ho! Ho! Secrets! Catch.' The logbook came crashing though the branches to land at their feet.

'Hey, cut it out,' yelled Joan. 'That's not funny.' She rescued the precious logbook, examining it carefully for damage.

But Mackey was gone again, out of the Crow's Nest, and climbing rapidly up through the canopy of leaves until they couldn't see him any longer. His voice floated downwards. 'Hey, I can see the sea – it's deadly up here.'

'He must be right at the top,' said Jonathan in wonder. 'I've never seen anyone climb so fast.'

'Who said he couldn't climb anyway?' demanded Felicity.

Mackey descended the tree at an even faster pace, sliding down the last bit like it was a greased pole.

'You never told us you could climb like that,' Jonathan accused.

'You never asked.'

'How did you learn when you had no trees in the city?' Muggins was looking at him with profound admiration.

Mackey shrugged. 'Shinning up drainpipes – same thing.'

Felicity was envious. Mackey wasn't any bigger than she was, and he could manage the Red Belly no bother. She would just have to try a bit harder.

Even Orla was impressed. 'I've never seen anything like it. You're brilliant.'

'He's the best climber in the whole gang,' declared Jonathan proudly, slapping Mackey on the back.

Joan was getting fed up.

'He's not in the gang yet,' she said.

'Of course he is. What are you talking about?'

'He hasn't done the initiation.'

'Don't be silly, there's no initiation,' said Jonathan, glaring at Joan.

'Oh yes there is. Remember Bully Girl?'

How could they forget? Last year the school bully had found out about their gang and insisted she was going to be part of it. So they had invented the initiation, and made it so hard that she would never be able to pass it. She had gone home in tears, having fallen at the first test, and they hadn't had any trouble with her since.

'That's different,' said Jonathan. 'That's only for people we want to keep out. Mackey doesn't have to do any initiation.'

'Oh well,' Joan shrugged, 'if he's afraid ... '

'I'm not afraid of anything,' growled Mackey. 'What do you want me to do?'

Jonathan rounded on Joan. 'Why are you trying to cause trouble? We all want Mackey in the gang.'

'I don't remember voting.'

Jonathan stared at her in disbelief.

'It's all right,' said Mackey. 'I'll do the initiation. Earn my place fairly.'

The rest of the gang looked anxiously at one another.

CHAPTER 4
THE INITIATION

'You don't have to,' said Orla. 'Really you don't. Joan is just being mean.'

They were all sitting around the Captain's Table arguing.

'I'm doing it, and that's that,' insisted Mackey.

'But we really don't have an initiation,' Jonathan explained. 'And those things we told Bully Girl to do were things we'd never do ourselves.'

'I'm doing it,' Mackey said stubbornly. 'Now, what's the first test?'

'Don't tell him.'

'To jump from a high place,' said Joan, challenge clearly in her voice.

'Did Bully Girl do that?'

'Yes, but she sprained her ankle and skinned her elbow.'

'Just show me the place.'

'This way.' Joan slid off her perch and marched away in the direction of the Red Belly, with Mackey in tow. The rest of the gang followed reluctantly.

On the edge of the Red Belly clearing, a fallen tree had come to rest propped against another tree at a steep angle. The fallen tree didn't have any branches at all low down; it formed a sloping walkway up into the other tree. The gang used this a lot in their tree-chasing, but they usually went up it crab-like, holding on to the trunk.

'You've got to walk up it without holding on,' Joan told him, 'and then jump from the place where the two trees meet.'

'OK,' said Mackey, not a bit put-out. He stood up on the tree-trunk, balancing with his arms stretched out like a tightrope walker. Then in one clear determined dash, he walked quickly right to the top.

Jonathan gasped in admiration. 'Did you see that? Isn't he great?'

'Let's see how great he is at jumping,' said Joan.

Orla looked worried. 'I hope he doesn't break a leg.'

'Will I go yet?' Mackey was waiting for their signal.

'Yes, go,' shouted Joan, before anyone could say no.

Mackey launched himself from the tree, landing on the ground in a perfect roll. He got up and calmly brushed the soil from his clothes.

'Hey, that was really something!'

'Brilliant!'

'How on earth did you do that?'

The gang were astonished – it was a perfect performance.

'Fella in the pub showed me,' said Mackey casually. 'He did parachute jumps – you have to learn how to fall properly. We used to practise from a shed roof.'

They were speechless with admiration – all except Joan, who was furious at all the praise that Mackey was getting. 'What about the next test?' she demanded.

'We can skip that,' said Jonathan quickly. 'I think Mackey has shown that he's more than fit to join our gang.'

'Rules are rules.'

'She's right. I want to do the test anyway.'

'But the next one wasn't really meant to be done at all.' Orla was frightened at the very thought of Mackey attempting it.

'Yes,' agreed Felicity. 'It was just a fantastic thing we decided on to make sure Bully Girl would fail.'

'What is it?'

'Don't anyone tell him.'

'It's to jump from one tree to another,' said Joan, 'way up at the very top.' She smirked at Mackey.

'Right. Where are they?'

'Over there.' Joan pointed out the two trees, growing side by side, very straight and tall. Their branches almost touched one another; almost, but not quite. 'See the long branch that overlaps one from the next tree?'

'The one really high up?'

'That's it. Well, you have to climb up and cross over to the next tree by that branch. There's a bit of a gap, so you have to jump.'

'OK,' said Mackey, quite unconcerned.

'You shouldn't have told him.' Felicity was looking at Joan in dismay. What had come over her friend?

'You'll fall and be killed,' said Muggins.

'No I won't.'

'It's too dangerous,' Felicity said. 'We play in the trees, but we never really do anything that dangerous ourselves – there's a limit!'

'Yes,' agreed Orla. 'You have to know where to draw the line.'

'I can do it, no bother.'

'It's silly. It's not worth the risk. Just forget it.'

'You'll get us all into trouble if you fall.'

Mackey laughed. 'But I won't fall, will I?'

With that, he walked over to the first tree and started climbing. They watched as he swung himself expertly upwards. He was a graceful climber as well as a swift one.

'He'd make a great mountaineer,' said Jonathan enviously.

And indeed, Mackey appeared to have no fear at all. He climbed out onto the high branch, holding on to another one overhead at first, then dropping down to straddle the branch he was on. The bough from the other tree was almost below him now.

He was very high up. If he fell, he wouldn't have a chance.

He sat still, considering the situation carefully.

The gang watched from below, necks craned back. Felicity could feel her heart thumping with alarm. Orla covered her face – 'Tell me when it's all over.' Jonathan was feeling slightly green himself, and that wasn't helped by Muggins babbling away beside him – 'He'll fall. He'll fall.'

'Shut up, Muggins. You're making us all nervous.'

Only Joan watched impassively, convinced he would flunk it at the last minute.

Mackey launched himself into the air. Felicity shut her eyes, unable to look.

'He's done it! He's done it! The so-and-so's done it.' Jonathan was jumping up and down with glee.

Felicity opened her eyes and saw that Mackey was hanging dangerously from the branch of the other tree. They watched as, hand over hand, he eased himself inwards until he could get a foothold on another branch beneath him. Once he was secure, he waved at them all below.

'Brilliant. Brilliant.' Jonathan was lost in admiration.

'Do you want me to do it again?' Mackey yelled.

'No!'

'No!'

'Don't!'

They were horrified, but Mackey just laughed. 'Only joking,' he shouted. He climbed swiftly down the tree again and cutting short their praises said, 'OK. What's next?'

'I think you've done enough.' Jonathan shot a warning look at Joan, who shrugged sulkily. It wasn't turning out like she expected.

But Mackey insisted – and finally they had to give in and tell him.

It wasn't anything dangerous this time, just a test of nerves.

'There's an old gate-lodge in the field behind the woods. The test is to spend the night there – by yourself.'

'Is that all?'

'Well, not quite. The lodge is haunted.'

'So? Who's afraid of ghosts?'

They all were, but nobody said so in the face of Mackey's complete unconcern.

'Right,' said Mackey. 'I'll do it next Friday night. It's school tomorrow and I can't be falling asleep on my first day. Can we go and take a look at the lodge now, though?'

Jonathan led the way through the woods and out to the field at the back. The gate lodge was at the far end of the field. Once upon a time it had formed part of a big estate, but now it stood in the middle of nowhere, on a path that was long overgrown with weeds and grass . Approaching it from this side, it looked completely intact, with the door and windows bricked up.

'Where's the way in?' asked Mackey.

'Around the back. Follow me.' Jonathan led the way.

From the other side, it was clear that part of the chimney-stack had fallen through the roof. Someone had removed bricks from one of the windows, leaving a space just big enough to climb into. They squeezed through one by one and stood inside.

'It's like a coffin,' said Mackey, 'with all those windows blocked up.'

They shivered. The place felt cold and damp in spite of the warm weather. They were standing in the main room. The ceiling had fallen in at one point, and rubble from the chimney-stack was scattered around. A huge collapsed roof beam hung down almost to the floor. Looking up, they could see through the hole in the roof.

'This is where I'll stay,' decided Mackey. 'I might get a bit of moonlight through that hole.'

The rest of the house consisted of two tiny rooms, but they couldn't see much as it was pitch black and they hadn't got a torch with them. They went back into the main room. There was nothing else there, apart from the fireplace.

'Look at the size of that,' said Mackey.

'It has one of those big chimneys where you can see the sky,' explained Felicity.

'Let's have a look.'

They all crammed into the fireplace and looked upwards.

'Wow! It's huge.' Mackey was impressed. 'You could climb up there no bother.'

'But it's filthy,' said Joan. 'Who'd want to?'

They got back out of the fireplace and Mackey decided where he was going to sleep – in the alcove beside it.

'I could light a fire too,' he said.

'That's cheating,' declared Joan. 'Makes things easier.'

'OK. I won't so.' Mackey looked at the others. 'How will you know when I'm going?'

'What do you mean?'

'Well, how do I tell you that I'm on my way?'

'We hadn't really got around to details like that,' admitted Jonathan.

Mackey thought for a bit. 'I know,' he said finally. 'I'll be out in the woods at midnight. My Ma is usually in bed by half past eleven. So you keep watch from your bedroom windows, and I'll give you a signal.'

'What sort of a signal?'

'With a torch. I got a real signalling torch from this fella in the pub. He taught me Morse code and all.'

'But where will you be when you signal?' asked Felicity, puzzled.

'Up the Red Belly.'

'But you can't climb the Red Belly in the dark.'

'Course I can. And you can all see the top of the Red Belly from your bedroom windows. So I'll give the OK signal at midnight exactly, and you'll know I'm on my way. O is three long flashes held for three seconds each, then a rest for three seconds, then a long flash, a short flash and a long flash for K. I'll repeat it three times just in case.'

'Sounds awfully complicated.' Muggins looked doubtful.

'Well, we'll see the flashes anyway,' Felicity pointed out. 'It doesn't matter if we don't understand them.'

'It's just as well I don't need to send you a message,' said Mackey in disgust. 'Everybody should know Morse code.'

Joan was getting annoyed again. 'How will we know you actually went to the lodge? I mean, you could easily cheat and just go back to bed again.'

'Someone will have to check,' said Jonathan.

'We could all go and check, for that matter,' Muggins suggested.

'Then I wouldn't be on my own, now would I?' said Mackey practically.

They all thought about this, but couldn't come up with any really good answer. Then Mackey grinned.

'I've got it. Leave it to me – I promise you that in the morning you'll know I've been there.'

'What are you going to do?'

But he wouldn't tell them ...

CHAPTER 5
A SIGNAL FROM THE WOODS

The following week seemed never-ending.

Mackey was getting on fine at school; he had settled in without any trouble. But everyone's mind was focused on Friday night.

'Why is it that time goes slowly when you don't want it to and fast when you do?' complained Jonathan to Felicity on Wednesday.

'I don't know,' said Felicity. 'I wish the holidays would hurry up and come too.'

But Friday came at last, and they went to bed that night in a state of high excitement. The excitement soon wore off, however, as they realised how hard it was to stay awake when you really wanted to.

'Come into my room,' suggested Jonathan, 'and we can keep each other awake.'

They played cards as the time ticked by ever so slowly. Felicity kept falling asleep sitting up, which she found rather funny. Jonathan was a bit better, but even he yawned so many times, and the card game dragged so much, that they were delighted to be able to abandon it completely as midnight drew near.

They went to the window and waited. All their bedrooms were at the back, so they knew that Joan and Orla and Muggins would be watching also.

'Nothing yet. I can't see a thing.' Jonathan was peering out, nose flattened against the glass.

'It's an awfully dark night,' said Felicity.

'There's too much cloud cover and no moon.'

'Mackey won't be able to find his way around.'

'He's got a torch, hasn't he? And he says it's a powerful one.'

'I suppose so.' Felicity didn't sound very convinced.

'There it is. I saw something.' Jonathan gave her a dig in the ribs.

'Ouch!'

'Ssssh ... you'll wake Mum and Dad. Look, there it is again.'

They pressed their faces to the glass, and sure enough, a long bright flash came out of the darkness. They counted the three seconds. Then another flash came.

'That's O. It's him all right,' whispered Jonathan.

'Well, who else would be up in the trees at this hour of the night?'

'Ssssh.'

They watched as there was a long flash, followed by a short flash, than another long one.

'That's K,' Jonathan murmured.

'I know.' Felicity had been reading Mackey's Morse code book too.

'He's going to repeat it all again.'

They watched as the series of flashes was repeated twice more.

'It's a wonder we can see it so well,' whispered Felicity.

'Well, it is a signalling torch. They have special reflectors to make them extra bright.'

'It's good all the same.'

They stared into the darkness, but no more signals came. They couldn't see anything outside, not even the outline of the top of the Red Belly against the sky. On moonlit nights it could be clearly seen. Felicity had her bed placed in such a way that she could always see it, even when she was lying down. And she never closed her bedroom curtains at night.

'He's gone. We'd better go to bed. I'm jaded.' Jonathan yawned sleepily.

'Night-night.'

Felicity went back to her own room and snuggled down, glad it wasn't she who had to face a night alone in the haunted gate-lodge.

☆☆☆

They slept late next morning, and could hardly eat their breakfast with the excitement.

Joan called to the door at half past ten, and Orla and Muggins shortly after.

'Any sign of Mackey?' asked Felicity.

'Of course not, he'll be in bed. He's probably been up all night,' said Orla.

'He said he was going to sleep,' Jonathan pointed out.

'Could you sleep in a haunted house? It's all very well being brave until you get in there, but then it's a different matter.'

'Will we go and call for him?' Jonathan was finding the tension unbearable.

'We'd better wait a bit, until half past eleven at least.'

They hung around the back garden, restless. Mackey's bedroom window had its curtains tightly closed.

'Will we throw stones at his window?' suggested Muggins.

'Don't! His Mum will hear.'

'It's a quarter past eleven ... let's call for him,' Jonathan said.

Unable to bear waiting any longer, the gang trooped up Mackey's garden path and knocked on the back door.

Mrs McCarthy seemed pleased to see them. 'He's not up yet. I don't know what's wrong with him this morning. I've called him three times already and he keeps falling asleep again. Up you go, the lot of you, and get him out of the bed.'

They ran up the stairs and knocked on Mackey's door.

'Mackey!'

'Mackey!'

There was no answer.

Jonathan turned the handle and walked in.

Mackey was lying in bed with his face to the wall. He didn't even move when they all crowded into his room.

'Mackey. Mackey!' Jonathan shook his shoulder.

'It's us. Wake up! We're dying to know how you got on,' said Felicity, plonking herself onto the bed.

There was a loud groan, and after a few seconds, Mackey rolled over to face them.

They gasped in horror.

The whole right side of his face was swollen black and blue, and his right eye was tightly shut.

'Do I look as bad as I feel?' His voice came out completely hoarse – he could barely speak at all.

'What happened?'

'How did you do that?'

'Oh, Mackey. You look awful.'

Mackey tried to sit up, but the effort proved too much and he lay back on the pillow, feeling the side of his face gently. His hands were very dirty and his pillow seemed to be damp.

'What happened?' asked Jonathan again.

There was a long pause before he answered, the words no more than a whisper ....

'The ghost got me.'

They digested this information in appalled silence. Mackey sat up and crawled slowly along the bed until he could see into the dressing-table mirror. He stared at himself for a few seconds, then crawled back into bed again.

He said nothing.

The silence was so unlike Mackey that the gang didn't know what to do or say.

Unfortunately, at that moment Mackey's Mum came up the stairs and straight into the room. She screamed when she saw Mackey, then became quite hysterical, ordering them all out. She shooed them down the stairs and out into the garden, locking the back door behind them.

They stood in the garden, bewildered, wondering what they should do. They saw Mackey's bedroom curtains being opened, and Mrs McCarthy waved her hand at them, telling them to go home.

They went into the woods and sat around the Captain's Table, feeling uncomfortable and guilty.

What had happened? What would Mackey say to his Mum?

It was awful just sitting there with all the questions buzzing around in their heads and no one to answer them.

'Why don't we go and check the gate-lodge?' suggested Felicity at last.

'Will it be safe?' asked Muggins fearfully.

'Well, there are five of us, and it's daylight – we were never afraid before.'

'Mackey said he'd leave us a sign. We could look for that,' said Orla. 'It's better than just sitting here.'

They were glad to have something to do. They walked listlessly through the woods and out into the field.

'Look,' shouted Felicity. 'Just look!' She pointed in the direction of the gate-lodge.

In big white letters, scrawled across the tiles of the roof, were the words: 'Mackey Was Here'.

'That's brilliant,' said Jonathan in admiration. 'Just brilliant. Trust him to think of something like that.'

'It's vandalism,' said Joan.

'Don't be silly. It's probably only chalk that will wash off in the first shower of rain.'

They walked through the long grass to the gate-lodge and went around the back.

'Well,' said Jonathan. 'Who's going in?'

There were no volunteers.

'One of us could just look in through the hole,' suggested Orla.

'The ghost might chop our heads off!' Muggins backed away in alarm. 'We need a periscope.'

'Well, we haven't got one, silly. It that the best you can come up with?' Orla looked at her brother in exasperation.

'I'll try and have a look,' offered Felicity bravely. Not being able to climb the Red Belly often made her volunteer for things the rest of the gang wouldn't do.

She put her face to the hole, but could see nothing. Then, in a burst of courage, she put her head and shoulders right through.

'Can you see anything?' Jonathan was hopping with impatience.

'Yes. Mackey's torch is on the ground, beside the fireplace.'

'Why would he leave his good torch behind?' Orla frowned.

'Probably dropped it when he saw the ghost, and ran,' said Jonathan.

'But he wrote on the roof – he must have stayed here until daylight to do that.'

The mystery deepened.

'Well, we'd better collect his torch anyway,' Jonathan decided. 'You go in and get it, Felicity.'

Felicity rapidly took her head back out of the hole. 'Why me?'

'Because you're the bravest,' declared Muggins.

'Oh ... all right.' Felicity reluctantly clambered in and collected Mackey's torch from the alcove. Then she climbed straight out again, having no desire to hang around.

CHAPTER 6
MACKEY'S STORY

There was no sign of Mackey for the rest of the day, or the next morning either.

The doctor came, and went, and still they had no news. They were afraid to knock on the door and ask how he was. Finally, after lunch, Mrs McCarthy sent word that they could all come and visit Mackey for a while. She let them in without saying anything.

'How is Mackey, Mrs McCarthy?'

'As well as he deserves to be,' his mother said grimly, and motioned them up the stairs.

Mackey was sitting up in bed, looking even more awful than he had the day before. His face had swollen up bigger, and was a medley of unbelievable shades – black and purple and green -right down to his chin.

'Hi, Mackey. We brought you stuff – lemonade and comics.'

'Thanks.' Mackey had hardly any voice.

'We were worried about you,' said Felicity.

'What on earth happened the other night?' Jonathan arranged himself on the bed.

'Close the door,' whispered Mackey, 'and make sure my Ma isn't around.'

Felicity went to look. 'It's OK. She's down in the kitchen.'

'Well, jam a chair against the door. I don't want her walking in on us again.' Mackey seemed in good form, in spite of his lack of voice and the way he looked.

'What happened, for heaven's sake.'

'I told you already. The ghost got me.'

'No, really!'

'Honest. Cross my heart. There I was, sleeping comfortably in the alcove, and I woke up with somebody trying to strangle me.'

'What!'

'You're joking!'

'I'm not. I wish I was ... and I don't even believe in ghosts,' croaked Mackey fervently. 'Listen to my voice. It's all hoarse. He damaged my windpipe ... I could hear it crunching ... there was something tight around my neck and I couldn't breathe. I thought I was going to die.' Mackey paused.

They were all listening in horrified fascination.

'What did you do?' asked Felicity.

'I started to pray like mad,' said Mackey. 'I was struggling something awful, when suddenly ... I broke free. I ran to get out, but it was pitch dark and I couldn't find my torch ... and I couldn't find the entrance either. I was bumping into walls and tripping over things ... and then I ran straight, whack, into the big roof beam ...and fell backwards into the fireplace. I knew it was the fireplace 'cause I could feel the air coming down. So I did the only thing I could think of to escape.' Mackey paused again, his voice almost gone.

'What?' chorused the others.

'Tell us ... oh, do go on,' entreated Felicity.

'I climbed the chimney.'

They stared at Mackey in disbelief.

'In the dark?'

'Yeah, it was awful. I had to wedge myself in and feel my way blind, but I was so afraid the ghost would grab hold of my legs from below that I did it in double-quick time. I was terrified out of my wits.'

'And what happened then?'

'I sat up on the chimney-stack all night.'

There was a short silence as the gang considered this. Finally Orla said what they were all thinking: 'But why didn't you just come home?'

'It was pitch dark,' explained Mackey. 'I tried to climb down, but I couldn't see the good bits and nearly fell through the hole in the roof. I knew if I fell back down there I'd be dead. I was going to do a parachute roll off the roof, but then I got to thinking ... what if I injured myself this time – fell on a brick or something – I'd have to lie there, and the ghost might come and get me – and I wouldn't be able to run. So I sat on what's left of the chimney and kept watch. Then when it got light, I came home.'

'We saw your message on the roof.'

Mackey grinned for the first time. 'Good, wasn't it? I nearly didn't bother, I was in such a state ... but I knew you'd never believe me if I didn't.'

'Maybe you dreamed it all,' said Joan.

'I did not! Sure I nearly choked to death!'

'You've got no marks around your neck.' Joan was inspecting Mackey closely.

'Well, I suppose ghost-chokes don't leave a mark. But he damaged my throat all right ... just listen to me.'

'But you were up on the roof all night,' pointed out Joan with maddening logic. 'You probably caught cold.'

'Oh, shut up, Joan. Leave him alone,' said Jonathan crossly.

'I think you're really brave,' Felicity sighed. 'It's the bravest thing I've ever heard of.'

Orla had been strangely silent. Now she was looking uncomfortable.

'Mackey,' she began. 'Look ... we're sorry ...'

'Why should you be sorry? It's my own fault. I wanted to do it.'

'Yes ... but the ghost ... we never dreamed he was dangerous.'

'How could you have known?'

'Well, we all knew the story, but we didn't think to tell you. The man who lived there once hanged himself. I thought a ghost would just ... sort of float around ... I never thought he'd try to hang you too.'

'Wow!' croaked Mackey, looking pleased. 'So I was right. It really was the ghost. That proves it.'

'What did you tell your Mum?'

'She thinks I was just messing around in the woods. I told her I ran into a tree in the dark. When I came home, I gave myself a wash, 'cause I was filthy from the chimney – I even stuck my head under the kitchen tap ... I want you to do me a favour. Look under the bed.'

Felicity got down on her hands and knees and peered under Mackey's bed.

'See the stuff under there? Pull it out, will you?'

Felicity crawled under the bed and retrieved a bundle of clothing wrapped in a plastic bag.

'Will you get rid of that for me? It's the stuff I was wearing when I went up the chimney. My Ma would kill me if she saw it, and I'd only have to explain ...'

'Will I wash them?' asked Felicity.

'No. Just dump them in a bin. They only mean trouble. My Ma will think they're lost or something.'

'OK so.'

'Look what else we brought you.' Jonathan produced the torch and handed it to Mackey.

'Hey, that's great! I thought it was gone for good.' He flicked it on and off to make sure it was still working, and looked pleased.

'How long will you have to stay in bed?' asked Felicity.

'I don't know. My Ma said she'd kill me if I tried to get up .... She's really mad at me. I hope it won't be long. It's dead boring here.'

───

✩✩✩

It was, in fact, another three days before Mackey was allowed up, and a full week before he went back to school. By then the swelling on his face had gone down completely, and the bruising had turned a nice mixture of pale lavender and green.

But now he was a fully-fledged member of the Red Belly Gang, and no one could dispute that.

Even Joan said it was all right.

What no one else knew, however, was that Jonathan had privately threatened her with being voted out of the gang, if she didn't lay off Mackey.

Chapter 7
Enter Harold

'Felicity!'

It was First Holy Communion Day, and everyone had the day off school.

Felicity had tidied her bedroom, hoovered downstairs, polished the dining-room and sitting-room, and cleared up the breakfast dishes.

She was just about to go out to play, when her mother called.

She ran back upstairs to the spare bedroom. Her mother was working at the computer. She looked up as Felicity came in.

'Felicity, be a pet and hang out the washing, will you?'

Felicity glanced out the window, where the empty clothesline was clearly visible in the back garden.

'But Jonathan was meant to do that,' she protested.

'Just do it, like a good girl.' Mrs Kelly was peering into the screen again, a frown on her face.

'But that's not fair! Jonathan gets away with murder! He never does anything!'

'Now Felicity, that's just not true.' Mrs Kelly turned around and gazed at her daughter in exasperation. 'He washes the car every week.'

'But that doesn't count,' said Felicity, outraged. 'Dad pays him for that ... Mum,' she went on, 'can we have a roster?'

'A what?'

'A roster of jobs. I've been thinking about it. I could do out a list of jobs and put our names against them for different days.'

'Really, Felicity. You'd think we had about ten children. There are only two of you, you know.'

'No,' explained Felicity. 'I mean all of us – you and Dad and Jonathan and me.'

Her mother stared at her. 'You can't put your father on a roster.'

'Why not?'

'You just can't!' Mrs Kelly, anxious to get back to work, lost her patience. 'I only asked you to hang a few clothes on the line.'

'But ...' began Felicity.

'You'd have it done ten times over in the time you've been standing there arguing.'

'But ....'

'No buts! Just do it!' Mrs Kelly turned back to her computer, and Felicity went downstairs to empty the washing machine.

She was out in the garden pegging up the last of the clothes when Joan arrived.

'I thought you were supposed to meet me at half past ten.'

'So I was,' mumbled Felicity, her mouth full of clothes-pegs. 'I got held up.'

'Orla can't come out. She has to mind the little ones. Muggins has gone to town with his Mum to get new clothes.'

Felicity spat out the pegs so she could talk. 'Is she on her own?'

'No, her Dad's there too. Orla says he's great with the kids, but he can't be left by himself because he won't change nappies or wipe bums.'

'I don't know how Orla does it.' Felicity wrinkled her nose.

'Well, I wouldn't,' said Joan. 'No way.' She quickly changed the subject. 'Did you see Harold Hanly?'

Harold lived across the road, and was making his First Holy Communion.

'No.'

'Guess what he was wearing?'

'Well, he was hardly wearing a white dress.'

'Not quite,' said Joan. 'He was wearing a white suit. I mean the real thing – a proper man's suit, with waistcoat and all – in pure white! He even had a pocket-watch on a chain. He showed it to me.'

Joan giggled. The impracticality of the whole thing was mind-boggling.

But then, Harold was different anyway.

Though he attended the local school, he was a bit of a loner. The other children walked to school, as it wasn't far, but Harold's mother drove him there and back – never offering anyone else a lift. He wasn't allowed to play out on Conker Road, though it was safe and quiet, or even in his own front garden. He was kept in the back garden, and every so often, selected children would be invited to come and play with him. His mother didn't take no for an answer, and didn't seem to understand that people of Felicity's age were too old to be asked.

No one liked it, for Harold was incredibly spoilt, and kept grabbing his toys back whenever anyone else tried to play with them. He also screamed and stamped when he wanted his own way and would hold his breath until he went quite blue – which fussed his mother so much that she ended up giving in. It wouldn't work in our house, Felicity thought ruefully.

'Let's go up to the church and watch them coming out,' suggested Joan.

Felicity put away the clothes-basket and they headed off. The church wasn't far away and the ceremonies were already over by the time they got there.

Harold was just getting into his parents' car outside the church, so Felicity only had a quick glimpse of him. Linking arms, the girls wandered among the First Communion children, admiring the style. Most of them were posing for photographs with their families.

'Just look at that one,' said Joan dreamily. The little girl was wearing tiered satin, like a ballgown, and a full-length veil. She had a white umbrella too – with frills.

Felicity sighed. 'I always wanted one of those.'

'Why didn't you get one for your own Communion?'

'My Mum said I should be thinking more about my prayers and not about silly fiddle-faddles.'

They sat on the railings watching the crowd gradually disappear. Finally all the children had gone and only Felicity and Joan were left in the church grounds. They set off home again.

As they came down Conker Road, Mrs Kelly was at the front door, looking very anxious.

'Felicity,' she called, when she spotted them, and beckoned with her finger.

Felicity ran on ahead, leaving Joan to follow.

'What's wrong?'

'I've been looking for you everywhere.' Mrs Kelly sounded harassed. 'We have a problem.'

Joan had come into the garden and was listening.

'It's little Harold. His Mum fell getting out of the car and may have broken her arm. She's gone to the hospital for an x-ray. She asked us to look after Harold until she gets back. Poor little fellow, on his First Communion day too.'

'And how long will that be for?' asked Felicity in horror, knowing what was coming next.

'Now Felicity, you know what hospitals are like. It will be a few hours at the very least. I want you to mind Harold, bring him to the shops or something.'

'Oh, do I have to?' wailed Felicity.

'Yes, you certainly do have to. I wouldn't ask you only I have something important to finish. Really, Felicity! I thought you'd be glad to help.'

Felicity looked rebellious. 'Why couldn't they bring Harold with them?'

'You know perfectly well he would only be a nuisance, and his mother was in great pain.' Mrs Kelly softened a little. 'Look, if I give you some money, will you bring him to the village and buy sweets – something, mind, that he won't get all over his suit. His Mum and Dad will be going visiting with him when they get back.'

'Can I buy sweets for Joan too?'

'Yes, I suppose so,' said Mrs Kelly. 'Here you are. Now don't let him buy ice lollies which will drip and stain his suit – and keep him out for a while, there's a good girl.'

She went inside to fetch Harold, while the girls looked with some comfort at the substantial amount that had been given to them to spend.

Harold came out of the house with his lip in an ominous pout.

He looked absolutely splendid in his white suit, a miniature little old man, watch-chain decorating the front of his chest. The girls distracted him by admiring him and asking to see the watch, which fitted into a special little pocket in the waistcoat. He took out the watch, which was in a silver case engraved with his initials in flowery writing. He pressed a little button and the lid flew open. The watch-face inside was breath-takingly beautiful. Delicate hands pointed to elegant Roman numerals.

'Can you read those numbers?' asked Felicity.

'Of course I can.' Harold proceeded to show them by reading the lot backwards.

'That's very good,' praised Felicity. 'It's a lovely watch. You can tell us the time whenever we want to know.'

In a better mood, Harold put the watch away, and they started for the village.

At the newsagents, Felicity let Harold select his own pick-and-mix sweets and put them in a paper bag. Harold took them without comment and popped one in his mouth. The girls chose their sweets, and having paid, left the shop with a bulging bag each. They sat on the seat outside for a while.

Harold was being very well-behaved, and Felicity had cheered up considerably. It wasn't going to be so bad after all, and her Mum would be in a good humour with her for helping.

People stopped to admire Harold, which pleased him greatly, and one or two even slipped him a coin, which pleased him even more. It was pleasant on the seat in the sunshine, and they filled in a useful twenty minutes before Harold became restless.

'I want a cream bun,' he mumbled, through a mass of sweets in his mouth.

Felicity looked at him. 'You're still eating. Finish what you have first.'

Harold transferred the sweets over to one side of his mouth where they made his cheek bulge, but left him free to talk.

'I want a cream bun!'

'But Harold, a cream bun is messy. You might dirty your suit.'

Harold's lip went down and his face got very red. 'I want a cream bun!'

'Sssh, Harold. People are looking.' Felicity anxiously tried to quieten him.

'Thump the little brat,' said Joan cheerfully.

But Harold was now standing up, stamping his feet in a rage. 'I want a cream bun! I want a cream bun!'

He started to gag on the sweets in his mouth and coloured dribbles ran down his chin. Felicity swiped at his chin with the sleeve of her sweater, successfully stemming the flow.

Harold screamed.

'OK! OK!' said Felicity fiercely, conscious that they were attracting a lot of attention. Some people had stopped and were watching suspiciously. 'You can have a cream bun.'

Harold immediately shut up and allowed Felicity to wipe his face properly. Down to the bakery they went, and Harold picked out the biggest one he could find.

The assistant wrapped a piece of plastic tissue around the bun, and started to put it in a bag.

'He's eating it now,' said Felicity. 'Harold, put your sweets away. You'll need both hands free.'

Harold obediently rolled up the paper bag of sweets and stored them away in his pocket. He took the big bun in his hands and licked at the cream oozing out.

Felicity paid for it and they left the shop, with Harold now safely distracted.

'Do you think we could make it home before he finishes that?' whispered Joan hopefully.

'We'd better.' Felicity looked grim. 'I've had enough of this.'

They walked in the direction of home, watching Harold warily as he worked his way through the cream bun. He even allowed Felicity to wipe the sugar off his face once or twice, and all was well until they reached the bottom of Conker Road.

The last bite went into Harold's mouth, and they stopped while he finished it off. Felicity cleaned his face again with the hem of her sweater, noting with satisfaction that his suit was still spotless. She could see Jonathan and Mackey up the road, and was anxious to divest herself of this responsibility as quickly as possible. She'd dump Harold back with her Mum and head for the woods.

But Harold wasn't going home just yet.

'I want to see the lake,' he stated flatly.

Felicity looked at him with horror. 'You can't. We're not allowed down there.'

At the bottom of Conker Road stood the entrance to an old estate, which had fallen into disuse. Up a long avenue was the shell of an enormous mansion, and behind that, an ornamental lake. They sometimes sneaked down to mess around, but as far as their parents were concerned, it was strictly out of bounds.

Harold's lip was trembling. 'I want to see the lake!' His face got very red.

'Harold,' said Felicity reasonably, 'we're not even allowed down there ourselves, so how can we bring you?'

Harold opened his mouth and howled, 'I – want – to – see – the – lake!' stamping his feet with each word.

'You can't. And that's all there is to it,' said Felicity crossly, reasonableness abandoned. She was thoroughly fed up with this spoilt little boy.

Harold started to scream, 'Want to! Want to! Want to ...' He suddenly ran out of words and turned blue, staring at them with huge eyes before collapsing on the ground, beating his fists on the pavement.

'Oh ... his suit,' exclaimed Joan, hands flying up to her face.

'He's choking ... Harold! Harold ... Are you all right?' Felicity dropped to her knees beside him, frightened.

Jonathan and Mackey came running down the road to see what the commotion was all about.

'What's wrong?'

'What happened?'

'He wanted to go to the lake,' said Felicity tearfully.

'And why don't you bring him?' asked Mackey.

Harold suddenly stopped his contortions and sat up.

Jonathan and Mackey helped him to his feet, and he stood quietly as they brushed him down, none the worse for his ordeal.

'The suit's a bit grubby,' observed Jonathan. 'I can't get all the dust off.'

'I want to see the lake.' Harold was looking at Mackey.

'Well, why not?' Mackey said. 'I haven't seen it yet myself.'

'We're not allowed down there,' Felicity repeated for the third time.

'We're not allowed a lot of things,' said Mackey slowly. 'If the little fella wants to see the lake on his Communion Day, he should see the lake.'

'Well, I'll come too then,' offered Jonathan.

Felicity looked desperately at the dirty suit. Bringing Harold home didn't seem such an attractive proposition any more.

'OK,' she said. 'Let's go.'

Chapter 8
At The Lake

They turned and went in the direction of the old estate.

The main avenue was very long – at least a mile, Jonathan reckoned – and the big house seemed only the size of a matchbox from this distance. The avenue was bordered on each side by a double row of trees, most of them over a hundred years old. They branched out in huge canopies overhead, or twisted down and dug their elbows into the ground, forming tree-tents.

Mackey wanted to stay and climb, and Harold was all set to do the same.

Felicity thought quickly. A grubby suit was one thing; a torn suit was quite another matter. 'We haven't time,' she said. 'If you want to climb, then we can't go to the lake – we'll have to walk fast as it is.'

So they settled for the lake.

It took a long time to get to the bottom of the avenue. The old house loomed large before them. It had looked quite beautiful from a distance, shining white in the sun, but this close they could see that all the windows and the door were bricked up, and the chimneys stood rawly against the skyline on their brick pillars. The roof was completely gone. There was a big notice in front: 'Trespassers Will Be Prosecuted'.

Mackey, of course, immediately looked for a way in, but couldn't find any. Felicity breathed a sigh of relief.

'Where's the lake?' inquired Mackey, having exhausted the possibilities of the house.

'That way.' Jonathan pointed. 'Follow me.'

They went around the back and into a stretch of woodland.

The path was level at first, then sloped steeply to the lake. They ran down the last bit, Jonathan and Mackey whooping like Indians, and Felicity had to grab hold of Harold in case he ran right into the lake itself.

It was quite a small lake, really. There was a sharp drop of about two feet down to the water, which was covered in thick green slime. Further along the bank was an ornamental boat-house, and out in the middle of the lake, a tiny island.

Harold knelt on the edge and leaned over, trying to touch the green stuff floating on top of the water.

'Get up!' said Felicity in alarm, grabbing hold of the tail of his jacket. 'I know, let's find a stick, and you can trail it in the water.'

They searched in the woods and found a long stick that was just right. Harold walked up and down the lake edge, happily poking at the slime.

Joan stood to one side, watching. She didn't really like it there. It was dirty, and had a stagnant smell.

Meanwhile Jonathan and Mackey had found other amusements.

Over to one side of the lake was a steep mud embankment, sloping down from the woods. On top was a stone watch-tower, three stories high, with large window openings on every floor.

The two boys crawled their way up the slope and climbed the stone staircase inside the tower. They appeared briefly at the ground-floor window, then the first-floor, and finally at the second-floor window, where they waved to Felicity and Joan and Harold far below.

Mackey leaned out the window, looking down at the almost sheer drop into the lake.

'Be careful!' called Felicity. 'Mind you don't fall.'

Mackey's answer was to climb up onto the window ledge, where he perched dangerously, clinging to the lintel overhead. Then bravado took over. 'Look!' he yelled. 'No hands!'

He took his hands from the lintel, and slowly stretched them out in front of him, for all the world as if he intended diving down into the lake.

Felicity couldn't bear to look. She closed her eyes tightly, afraid to shout another warning in case it made Mackey lose his balance.

Joan gasped.

Felicity waited for the awful catastrophe she knew was coming.

There was a sudden loud splash and a terrible high-pitched screaming.

Felicity opened her eyes and looked up, expecting to see the window empty. But Mackey was still there, now holding on tightly to the window edge.

Confused, Felicity looked around. Harold had fallen into the lake, and was struggling face down in the slime.

Joan was screaming at the top of her voice: 'He'll drown! He'll drown!'

Felicity didn't hesitate – she jumped in to the rescue.

Her knees hit her chin with a resounding whack, and she was thrown backwards into the water, which immediately filled her nose and mouth with disgusting sludge. She scrabbled frantically to right herself, and discovered she was sitting up in no more than a foot of water.

Harold sat beside her, looking bewildered, a sheet of green slime draped over his head and shoulders.

Felicity fingered her chin, where a big lump was rising fast. She stood up, feeling extremely foolish.

The boys had come down from the tower at full speed. Sliding down the mud-bank on his bottom, Mackey was the first to reach the lake. He danced along the edge, shaking his fist at Harold. 'You fizzin' eejiit! Whatcha have to go and do that for? We'll all be killed!'

Harold just stared back.

'Are you all right?' asked Felicity softly.

He nodded.

She helped him up and over to the lake's edge, where they were pulled out by Jonathan and Mackey.

Harold stood there dripping, the slime slowly moving down his suit, leaving green trails behind it. A large red and blue stain had appeared on the

pocket of his jacket, and rapidly ran down the leg of his trousers.

'The sweets,' groaned Felicity in despair.

Harold extracted the bag of sweets from his pocket, but it burst in his hands and the contents fell down the front of his suit.

Felicity was shivering with the cold and shock.

Joan just stood there, while Jonathan and Mackey looked at one another for inspiration.

'Maybe we can clean him off a bit,' said Jonathan, bending down to pick up a handful of leaves. He rubbed at the slime, and the leaves crumbled into a brown mess.

'Leave him,' said Felicity miserably. 'You're just making it worse ... Let's go home.'

They didn't talk much on the way back.

Halfway down the avenue, Harold suddenly stopped and searched in his inside pocket. He took out the silver watch on its long chain. They had all forgotten about the watch.

Harold opened the lid, and a small gush of water came out. It looked OK, apart from being wet, but the minute hand was no longer moving ... Harold put it to his ear. 'It doesn't tick any more,' he said sadly, and put the watch back in his pocket.

They continued on their way home. Felicity was thankful that Harold was taking it all so well, and wasn't crying and screaming the way he usually did.

As they turned up Conker Road, Harold's mother and father were just getting out of their car. Mrs Hanly had her arm in a sling. Mr Hanly saw them first, and the look of horror on his face made

Mrs Hanly turn to look too. She gave a loud cry, and clutched the car door for support ....

☆☆☆

The next few hours were not pleasant.

The next few days were not pleasant either, for that matter, as Felicity faced endless recriminations from her mother – and the prospect of no pocket money for weeks.

'It's not fair! It wasn't all my fault,' she wailed.

'Felicity,' her mother explained patiently, 'I didn't ask Jonathan to mind Harold ... I didn't ask Ignatius to mind Harold ... I asked you.'

'But it wasn't even my idea to go to the lake!'

'You don't have to do what other people suggest,' pointed out Mrs Kelly, 'and you know quite well you're not allowed down there yourself without an adult, let alone bring Harold.'

'But ...'

'But nothing. You have to learn a sense of responsibility. If I ask you to do something, I expect you to do it.'

Felicity was silent. What could she say? Her mother was stopping her pocket money to help pay for the expensive one-hour cleaning of Harold's clothes ... and the watch was a total write-off. Felicity felt bad about the watch. She decided to give Harold her new Swiss army penknife to make up for things, but when she went to get it from her dressing-table, it was missing. She turned her whole bedroom upside down, but couldn't find it anywhere.

☆☆☆

The only winner in all of this was Harold.

The truth was he didn't care about the suit, or even the watch.

He had just had the first real live adventure of his sheltered little life – and found himself a hero ...

At school, he had to tell the story over and over again. Somehow it changed and grew with the telling and re-telling, until eventually, everybody knew how Harold had jumped into the lake in his First Communion suit to save Felicity's life.

Everyone wanted to see the watch, whose insides had rusted spectacularly. Mrs Hanly was greeted by the astonishing sight of a constant stream of children knocking on her door, all wanting Harold to come out and play on the road.

She was so surprised that she let him.

Chapter 9
Holidays At Last

'Holliers at last!'

'Two whole months!'

'No more English, no more French ...' started Felicity.

'No – more – sitting – on – the old – school – bench!' shouted Joan and Orla together, rolling on top of her as they all collapsed into laughter.

The girls were lying on a rug in Joan's back garden, taking advantage of the first really hot summer weather.

They were planning a picnic for next day.

'We haven't been to the river since last summer,' said Orla, 'and it's not as if it's that far away.'

'Some things are just holiday things,' Felicity declared. 'That's one of them. If we went all the time then it wouldn't be special.'

'And we wouldn't look forward to it so much,' agreed Joan.

'What'll we bring?'

'Jam sandwiches,' said Felicity. 'They're the only ones that still taste nice when they're hot and squashy.'

'Peanut butter is good too,' Joan decided.

'I like banana best,' said Orla.

'Yuck!' Joan wrinkled her nose. 'They go all brown and horrid.'

'I know, but they still taste the same. I close my eyes when I'm eating them.'

'Well, we're definitely bringing firelighters this time,' Felicity insisted. 'We spent all day trying to light the campfire last year.'

'My Dad's got a bag of charcoal in the shed,' said Orla. 'We'll bring some of that too – there's not much wood down by the river.'

'And lots of potatoes for baking.' Felicity felt her mouth watering at the very thought.

Orla nodded. 'We should get everything ready tonight so that we can start really early in the morning.'

'I'm jolly well going to make sure that Jonathan makes his sandwiches this time,' Felicity said. 'Remember last year he didn't bother, then went and ate most of mine?'

Joan and Orla laughed, recalling the fight that had ensued.

They lay on the rug, enjoying the sunshine. Then the back door of Joan's house opened and a beautiful smell came wafting out.

'My Granny's making a batch of rock buns for us all.'

'Yummy!'

'Three cheers for Dorcas!'

Joan's Granny insisted on the gang calling her Dorcas. She said that she had a name, and wasn't a label. The gang were a bit embarrassed at first, as it seemed sort of disrespectful, but they did as she asked – all except Joan, who refused, saying she wanted a Granny like everyone else.

Joan's mother worked full-time and her father was away at sea for months on end, so Dorcas lived with them and kept house. She had a house of her own, though, not far away, which was let for the moment. She planned to return to it when Joan got a bit older.

Dorcas came out into the garden, carrying a plateful of freshly-baked buns. 'Anyone want to test the survival rations?' She glanced around. 'Where are the rest of the crew?'

'Looking at some stupid wrestling magazine,' said Joan. 'We're not going to fetch them either – they're gone and left us to do all the planning for tomorrow.'

'Do you think you could manage these by yourselves then?'

Joan grinned at her Granny. 'Could we what! Just watch us.'

And the three of them launched themselves on the steaming plate of rock buns.

☆☆☆

The boys were up the Red Belly.

'Wow! Brilliant!'

'Just look at that hold!'

'And this one too,' said Mackey, showing them one of the many illustrations in his wrestling magazine. He knew it cover to cover.

'Did you ever see those big fellows on TV?' asked Muggins. 'They jump on each other and everything.'

'That's not real wrestling!' Mackey was scathing. 'That's just for show. They're pretending. Proper wrestling is serious stuff.'

'I'd love to learn how to do it.' Muggins was staring wistfully at the pictures.

'Sure I can teach you, no bother,' said Mackey. 'I know all about it. Fella in the pub showed me – he gave me loads of magazines too. Look, you start from this position here ....' He pointed to one of the illustrations.

'And you grab your opponent like this,' Jonathan interrupted, flinging his arm around Mackey's neck from behind, and locking it tightly against his throat.

Mackey struggled and kicked as his air supply was suddenly cut off, and Jonathan had to let go again as the two of them nearly fell out of the Red Belly.

'Stupid eejit!' roared Mackey. 'That's an illegal hold – neck locks are out. You could have killed me!'

Jonathan looked sheepish. 'I didn't know. I thought that's what you did.'

'Amateurs,' scoffed Mackey. 'You haven't a clue. I'd better give you a few lessons. Let's get down out of here ... no, wait.' He stopped suddenly, and his face lit up with mischief. 'You know this picnic tomorrow? ... Fellas, I've just had the deadliest idea ...'

CHAPTER 10
THE PICNIC

The gang set off early next morning on their journey to the river. They had decided to walk instead of getting the bus – that was Mackey's idea.

'We've got all day,' he said. 'Besides, we can spend our bus money on ice-cream.'

Felicity and Jonathan wore small rucksacks that they had got for Christmas. Joan had one too. Orla and Muggins used their schoolbags, and Mackey had a canvas satchel from Army Bargains.

Everything they needed for the day out had been crammed into these – except for the firelighters, which had been the source of some argument as nobody wanted to carry them.

'They'll make our sandwiches stink,' Joan protested.

Felicity finally solved the problem by putting three firelighters in a plastic bag and hanging it from the outside of her rucksack.

The day was hot, and by the time they reached the village near the river they were gasping for ice-cream. They bought huge cones, with chocolate flakes stuck in the middle, and sat outside the shop licking them, to have a rest.

'Are we nearly there?' asked Mackey. 'I'm dead.'

'Well, it was your idea to walk,' Orla pointed out.

'I didn't know it was so far – we must have walked ten miles.'

'A slight exaggeration. Haven't you ever hiked before?' Jonathan was pleased to find that there was *something* they could do better than Mackey.

'Once I went up the mountains with the scouts. I was dead after that too.'

'It's not far now,' said Felicity. 'We have to go up to the railway bridge, then about half a mile further on to the river.'

'Somebody carry me!' They all laughed at the pathetic look on Mackey's face.

Ice-creams finished, they set off again, up the hill to the station. Over the bridge they went, along a gently curving road, then downhill again. Suddenly the fields were spread out before them, unrolling to the far horizon. To the right, a steep embankment led down to their favourite field – and the river, which was really no more than a stream.

'Race you all,' yelled Jonathan.

They scrambled down the bank, tiredness forgotten.

The best place was halfway up the field. Here there were deep pools in the river, as well as shallows for paddling. They dumped their bags on the ground, threw off their runners, and sat on the river-bank cooling their feet in the water.

'Oh .... this is just bliss,' said Joan, closing her eyes in ecstasy as she swished her feet around.

They spent the morning fishing for tiddlers. They had brought jam-jars with string around the tops, and fishing nets made out of wire hangers and old nylon tights. It was a satisfying occupation, and the little fish were surprisingly hard to catch, darting away at the first sign of a shadow on the water. But by lunchtime they each had a good jar-full. Felicity never kept hers – she liked to watch them swimming around the jam-jar, but always returned them to the river before she went home.

'Let's have lunch,' said Muggins. 'I'm starving.'

'We'd better build a fire first and put in the potatoes,' Felicity said. 'They'll take ages to do – but we don't want them 'til later on anyway.'

They took stones from the river and arranged them in a circle, with firelighters in the middle. Kindling and old leaves were gathered from a clump of bushes at the end of the field and heaped inside the circle.

This produced an instant blaze when lit, and Orla quickly piled the charcoal on top. The potatoes were carefully pushed into the fire one by one – it was too much trouble waiting for it to heat up properly.

That done, they sat down to eat their sandwiches. They were ravenous, and made short work of the food they had brought – including Dorcas's rock buns.

Afterwards, they played rounders. It was a particularly boisterous game, with much argument about cheating, and they fell to the ground in a heap at the end of it, quite exhausted.

'I'm going to lie here forever,' said Felicity. 'I'm too tired to move.'

But five minutes later, after swigs of their remaining lemonade, they were all fine again.

'What'll we do next?' asked Orla.

The boys exchanged meaningful glances, and there was a slight pause.

'We're going to give a demonstration of wrestling,' said Muggins proudly. 'Mackey's been teaching Jonathan and me.'

'You can go first,' offered Jonathan. 'I'll be referee.'

Mackey and Muggins got into position facing one another, at the ready. They danced around, each watching for an opportunity to make the first move. Then Mackey dived for Muggins's right leg, grabbed his ankle, and in one neat movement had him completely off balance. Muggins ended up flat on his back.

Mackey quickly sat on him, and pinned both his arms to the ground.

' ... Eight, nine, ten, out,' yelled Jonathan.

'That's not fair!' howled Muggins. 'You didn't give me a chance to show my counter-move.'

Mackey smirked.

'My turn,' said Jonathan.

Muggins was looking disgruntled.

'You're referee now,' Jonathan pointed out. 'You can do another move in a few minutes.' Muggins cheered up a bit.

Jonathan and Mackey faced each other in a half-crouch. Jonathan made a grab at Mackey, but he slipped away completely and Jonathan fell to the ground. Mackey lunged for him, and Jonathan rolled over, trying to prevent Mackey from pinning him down. Soon the two boys were a tangle of arms and legs, rolling over in a series of moves and counter-moves. Mackey got Jonathan in a leg-lock from behind, then threw his right arm around

Jonathan's neck and held him there so that he couldn't move. Jonathan went limp in his arms.

'Let him go!' shrieked Orla. 'You're choking him!'

Mackey held on for another few moments before reluctantly releasing his hold.

Jonathan lay on the ground, a terrible rasping sound coming from his throat. His face turned very red.

'Jonathan! Jonathan! Are you all right?' Felicity knelt down beside him. There was no movement from him at all now, and he didn't seem to be breathing.

'He's dead! He's dead! Do something! Do something!' Joan was distraught. Mackey and Muggins just stared at her.

'Get an ambulance,' she screamed.

'Where?'

'Oh, fools! Fools!' Joan turned and ran off down the field towards the embankment.

Orla dropped down on her knees beside Felicity. 'Let me. I know the Kiss of Life.'

She pinched Jonathan's nose and clamped her mouth down on his, blowing gently. There was a choking, spluttering sound, and Jonathan's hands came up to shove her away.

'Get off me,' he roared, as he pushed her to one side, then sat up, laughing hysterically.

Muggins burst into cackles and couldn't stop.

Mackey was laughing too, rolling around the grass and beating his fists on the ground. 'Oh...! The funniest thing! Did you see her face?' He laughed and laughed and laughed, until Orla gave him a kick to stop him.

'You mean it was all a joke?'

'Yeah. Great, wasn't it? ... We had you rightly fooled.'

'Yeah, great,' said Orla sarcastically. 'And Joan has gone for an ambulance, and probably the police as well.'

Jonathan stopped laughing and looked over in the direction of the road.

'Go on.' Orla pushed him. 'You'll have to go after her.' When Jonathan appeared reluctant to move, she taunted, 'Afraid you won't be able to catch her?'

Jonathan got up quickly and ran towards the embankment.

'I'm going too,' said Felicity. 'She'll be rightly mad at him!'

By the time Felicity got to the road, Jonathan was far ahead, and Joan had already disappeared over the brow of the hill. Felicity ran and ran and ran, until she thought her lungs would burst. Up the hill, and along the road to the station. The curve of the road meant she couldn't see how far ahead Jonathan was.

She came out onto the last stretch and saw Jonathan standing on the railway bridge by himself, looking over the wall into the station.

She finally caught up with him, puffing for breath. 'Where's Joan?' She could hardly get the words out.

Jonathan pointed at the ticket office.

The office had a big window in front. They could see Joan sitting on a chair inside; the station-master was talking to her. Then he turned and picked up the telephone.

'What'll we do?' asked Felicity in alarm.

'I don't know.'

They watched as the station-master held a conversation on the phone, then put it back down again.

'We'll have to tell him,' said Jonathan urgently. 'Own up. I'll go. You wait here.'

He walked down the path to the ticket-office, and knocked on the side door. The station-master opened it.

'Please, sir, I want to talk to my friend – she's in here.'

'Come in.' The station-master stood aside to let Jonathan pass, then latched the door behind him. Joan looked quite faint at the sight of Jonathan, and her mouth opened and closed as she tried to speak.

'This young lady says somebody's dead.' The station-master sounded grim. 'I've sent for the police.'

'Nobody's dead. It's all a mistake.' Jonathan was shifting uneasily from foot to foot.

The station-master considered him carefully. 'Well, she's in a state of shock,' he said at last. 'She must have seen something. You'd better wait here until the police arrive.'

Jonathan looked at Joan in horror, as the station-master sat down on a chair beside the door.

They were trapped.

CHAPTER 11
RUN FOR IT!

Meanwhile, Felicity was watching from the bridge.

At first, when Jonathan didn't come out, she thought he was just taking a long time to explain. Then it dawned on her that he was, in fact, a prisoner.

She knew it was up to her now, and she had to move fast.

She walked calmly down to the ticket window and rapped on the glass.

The station-master got up, and came forward to attend to her.

'Please,' said Felicity, 'could you tell me how much it costs to bring a bicycle to Killarney on the train?'

'From where?'

'From here.' Felicity tried to look past him at Jonathan, but the station-master was blocking the way. She only hoped Jonathan would have the wit to understand what she was doing.

The station-master took down a book and started to leaf through it.

Jonathan suddenly realised what Felicity was up to. He grabbed hold of Joan, and pulled her towards the door. In a second they were free, and running for the bridge. Felicity ran after them as fast as her legs would carry her.

'Come back! Come back!' The station-master was at the door, shouting, but he couldn't follow, as he wasn't allowed to leave the station unattended.

The three of them ran for their lives – Joan far ahead, Jonathan trying desperately to catch up, and Felicity trailing behind, terrified, expecting every minute that a police car would pull up beside her to take her off to jail.

By the time she reached the field, the gang were on the move. Mackey and Muggins were already halfway across to the only shelter-spot around – a thick clump of low bushes by the wall at the bottom of the field.

'Put out the fire,' Orla shouted to Jonathan, picking up the rest of the bags.

Jonathan grabbed two of the jam-jars.

'No! No!' screamed Felicity in anguish. 'You'll fry the tiddlers.'

'Oh, do it yourself then!' Jonathan put the jar down, grabbed his own bag, and ran off after Mackey.

Joan followed, leaving Felicity and Orla to deal with the fire.

They ran to the river and emptied out all the fish, then filled the jars with water again, which they poured onto the charcoal. It sizzled and turned grey.

'Pity about the potatoes,' said Felicity.

'Quick, let's go!'

The two of them took off after the others, with anxious glances back to the road in case they were caught on open ground. They reached the bushes together and squeezed in underneath. Thorns tore at their hands and faces and clothes.

'Ouch! Ouch!'

'Ssssh!'

'Stop shushing us,' said Felicity crossly. 'There's no one here yet.'

She came to a halt beside Mackey. He was lying on his tummy, and could see out through a small gap, right over to the road. She changed position so she could see out too. The rest of the gang were squashed back as far as they could get.

'Do you think we can be seen?' asked Orla.

'No, we're OK here.'

'My face is all scratched,' complained Joan.

'I'm scratched too,' said Muggins, and indeed, there was blood running down his cheek.

'We're all scratched,' snapped Jonathan, 'so stop complaining.'

'Whose idea was this anyway?'

'Something's happening.' Mackey's voice was urgent.

Felicity pressed close so she could see out as well. 'A police car! With two policemen. It's stopped on the road.'

They watched as one of the policemen got out and scanned the field for a minute. Then he walked down the embankment, over towards the river, and followed its course across the field.

'He's found the fire,' whispered Mackey.

The policeman was standing by the ring of stones. He crouched down and felt for the heat with his hand. Then he stood up, and looked all around him.

'He's staring this way,' said Felicity.

'Look out. He's coming....Dead quiet, everyone.'

Felicity and Mackey put their heads to the ground and listened for footsteps. They couldn't hear a thing, except a slight swishing of grass.

Ages went by, and Felicity chanced a look. She nearly fainted. Less than three feet away were the trouser bottoms and shoes of the policeman.

He was standing still, beside a clump of brambles. She closed her eyes, hardly daring to breathe. When she chanced a look again, the policeman was already halfway back across the field.

'He's going!'

'Don't move,' warned Orla. 'They'll still be watching.'

They lay in silence for a few minutes.

'What's happening?' asked Muggins plaintively, from his position behind everyone else.

'He's back in the police car ... It's moving off!'

'Hooray!' shouted Jonathan, and there was a general sign of relief.

'Hooray nothing,' said Orla. 'What are we going to do now?'

'What do you mean?'

'Well, the police car will have gone on up the back road. We can't stay here, and we can't go home by the station either or we'll be caught on the bridge.'

'So what do we do?'

Orla frowned thoughtfully.

'We'll have to go home by the back road,' she said at last, 'but keep to the ditches, in case the police car returns.'

'But that's miles out of our way,' wailed Felicity.

'Anybody else have a better suggestion?'

'I wish I could fly,' said Muggins wistfully.

'Don't be stupid.' Orla looked around to see if there were any more ideas. There weren't. 'Well, we'll have to stay put here for a while anyway, in case they're waiting up the road for us to show ourselves.'

'How long will we have to wait?' asked Joan.

'I don't know.'

They lay in their hiding-place for ages, getting more and more fed up. At last, Orla decided: 'It should be safe now, but somebody will have to check the road before we all come out.'

'I'll go,' said Mackey. 'The station-master hasn't seen me.'

He crawled out of hiding, and ran across the field to the road. He disappeared out of sight for a few minutes. Then he came back and gave them the all-clear signal.

They squeezed thankfully out of their hiding-place and brushed themselves down.

'Look at my arms.' Joan held them out for inspection. The scratches had turned to long red weals, raised up like hives. She gingerly felt the ones on her face.

The gang looked at one another ruefully – they were all in the same condition.

'Better move,' said Orla briskly. 'We've a long way to go.'

'Can't we have our potatoes first?' asked Muggins, looking hopefully across to the campfire.

'We haven't time.'

'We could bring them with us,' Muggins persisted.

'Oh, all right then. But hurry up!'

Muggins ran across the field to the campfire and recovered the potatoes. They were still hot, but covered in wet ashes. He put them in his bag and hurried back to the others.

'Let's go,' said Orla.

☆☆☆

The journey home seemed endless.

They kept to the ditches as much as possible, and every time a car came along, they had to throw themselves flat, or dive through gaps in the hedges if the ditches weren't deep enough. It was an exhausting business, and tempers grew very thin indeed.

'We shouldn't have spent our bus money,' Muggins moaned.

'What's that got to do with anything?' Jonathan said crossly. 'There are no buses on this road anyway.'

'Great picnic.' Mackey was being sarcastic. 'Are all your outings like this one?'

'Who caused the trouble in the first place?'

'Well, I didn't.'

'Yes you did!' spat Joan.

'I did not. You made all the fuss. Stupid spoilsport.'

Joan went for him, and caught hold of his hair. Mackey grabbed Joan's hair, and they scrabbed viciously at one another.

'Stop it, you two!' Jonathan managed to separate them after a bit of a scuffle.

'What about our potatoes?' suggested Muggins, unconsciously defusing the situation.

They sat in a field and Muggins did the share-out. The potatoes were extremely dirty, but still warm and cooked right through. As they bit into them, their faces and hands got covered in black ash, which defied all attempts to wipe off again. They were starving. It was hours since lunch-time.

'These are gorgeous,' sighed Felicity. 'Imagine! Only for Muggins we would have left them behind.'

'Three cheers for Muggins!'

'Hip-hip-hooray ....'

'Ssh,' said Orla. 'The police might hear us.'

☆☆☆

They were very late getting home.

Mr Kelly had already finished his tea when Felicity and Jonathan came in. He viewed them with disbelief.

'What have you two been up to? I thought you were going on a picnic?'

'We did,' said Jonathan.

'You could have fooled me. You look like you've been on army manoeuvres.'

'We were too,' muttered Felicity under her breath.

'Well,' said Mrs Kelly cheerfully, 'as long as you had a good time ...'

They didn't look as if they'd had a good time, but then, what did parents know?

She sent them upstairs to shower, with instructions not to appear down again until they were squeaky clean.

CHAPTER 12
A VISIT FROM THE POLICE

Next morning, while Felicity and Jonathan were having breakfast, there was a knock on the front door.

'Who's that at this hour?' wondered Mrs Kelly as she went out into the hall to answer it.

There was the sound of voices, then somebody being invited in, the door closing, more voices.

Felicity and Jonathan had stopped eating now, alert to danger.

Felicity slipped out of her chair and opened the door to the hall a tiny crack.

She closed it again quickly, and came and sat down, her face suddenly very white.

'It's a policeman,' she whispered.

They stared at each other in panic. They could hear the policeman being shown into the sitting-room.

The kitchen door opened, and Mrs Kelly came in, looking angry. She beckoned with a finger. 'Felicity, will you come here a moment, please.'

Felicity got up and followed her to the sitting-room.

'This is Guard Whelehan,' said her mother. 'He's come to see you.'

He was a big policeman, uniform full of shiny buttons, with a fat leather belt around his waist. He had a notebook and pen in one hand, and he frowned severely as he looked at her. 'Well now, young lady, and what have you got to say for yourself?'

Felicity tried to bluff it out. 'About what?'

'Now, Felicity,' said her mother crossly, 'Guard Whelehan has told me all about it – how you fed a lot of stories to the station-master about someone being murdered, and got him to call out the police-car.'

Felicity said nothing – what could she say? That it wasn't her? Then they would want to know who it was. It would mean telling on Joan, and she couldn't do that.

She stood fidgeting and looking down at the patterns on the carpet, as both her mother and Guard Whelehan tried to get her to talk. Felicity remained silent.

Her mother was totally embarrassed. 'I don't know what's got into her, Guard. Look, I'll get my son. He's Felicity's twin. He may be able to shed some light on the whole business.'

She went out of the room, and Felicity heard her opening the kitchen door. She was back in a minute. 'Felicity, do you know where Jonathan is?'

Jonathan, the rat! He'd run off and left her to face the music.

Felicity couldn't believe it. She just stared at her mother with an agonised expression.

'Sorry, Guard. I'll just give him a shout. He can't be gone far. He was in the kitchen a few minutes ago.' She went out again, and they could hear her calling from the back door. 'Jon-a-than!'

'Jon-a-than!'

She called six times in all, before coming back.

Of Jonathan there was no sign.

Felicity had been thinking hard in the meantime, and something didn't quite add up. How had the policeman got her name? The station-master didn't know her, and nobody else had been around.

'Why do you think it was me?' she asked hopefully. Maybe he had made a mistake.

The policeman opened his hand. There on his palm lay a penknife with the name 'Felicity Kelly' scratched deeply along its surface.

'We found it in the ticket office. It didn't take too long to check out where you lived. There are not many people around with a name like that.'

Felicity felt sick. Jonathan again! She had lost that penknife weeks ago. The only reason she had her name scratched on it in the first place was so Jonathan couldn't take it and claim it was his own.

Felicity knew she was lost. There was no point in saying anything now. To prove her innocence she would have to get everybody else into trouble. So she remained silent through all the questioning ... and questioning ... It was most unpleasant.

Finally Guard Whelehan gave up any notion of extracting information from her, and launched into a lengthy sermon instead. At the end of it he told her, 'You're lucky, you know, that I'm not going to press charges. Calling out a police-car for fun is an indictable offence.'

Felicity didn't know what that meant, but it sounded ominous.

'Next time I won't be so lenient.' He wagged a warning finger at her.

Then her poor mother had to put up with being lectured on her duties as a parent, and her obvious lack of control over her offspring. It didn't put Mrs Kelly in a very good humour either.

After the policeman had gone, she went on and on about how Felicity had shamed her. She refused to allow her out for the rest of the day, setting her work to do in the house instead.

It was all so unfair!

☆☆☆

When Jonathan finally turned up, he was unrepentant.

'You left me to take all the blame,' said Felicity fiercely.

'Well, I didn't do anything – it was all Joan's fault. You hardly expected me to stay and tell on her?'

And what could Felicity say to that?

CHAPTER 13
A LETTER FROM AFRICA

'Hey, you lot! Letter from Zambia! Who wants a look?' Jonathan waved the letter in the air.

'Me first,' squealed Joan, grabbing it quickly.

Jonathan and Felicity parked themselves down comfortably on the Captain's Table. They had already read the letter over breakfast.

'Is that the first one?' asked Mackey.

'No, Dara's written before,' Felicity replied. 'He told us all about where he lives. He has bananas in his back garden ... and stick insects, and chameleons ... and a huge ant-hill for playing on beside his house.'

'What about the ants?'

'An empty one, silly. It's like a little mountain. He sent us photos.'

' ... And now he's been on safari too,' exclaimed Joan, just coming to that bit in the letter.

'Lucky ducker,' said Mackey fervently. 'I'd love to go to Africa and see all the lions and tigers and elephants.'

'There aren't any tigers in Africa,' observed Jonathan.

'There are so.'

'There aren't.'

'How would you know anyway?'

'Everyone knows that.' Jonathan had only just read it somewhere, as a matter of fact, but had no intention of letting on.

'It must be lovely to live in a jungle, all the same,' Mackey said. 'Dara's steeped.'

'There aren't any jungles in Zambia,' said Jonathan knowledgeably.

'Who says?'

'Dara says. He says Zambia is all bush.'

'What's that?'

Jonathan shrugged. 'Small bushes, I suppose.'

'And what do the giraffes eat then, Mr Smartie-Pants?'

'Well...' Jonathan was getting a bit out of his depth. 'They must have some trees too.'

Joan, still reading the letter, let out a shriek – 'He says he was charged by a rhino!'

'I know,' said Jonathan enviously. 'Some people have all the luck.'

'He's in a wildlife club at school too,' enthused Felicity, 'with a funny name – I've forgotten it already ... spell it out, Joan.'

Joan shuffled back a page and read, 'Chon-go-lo-lo.'

'Chongololo .... Chongololo.' They rolled the unfamiliar sound around their mouths, giggling.

'Dara says it's a sort of big black worm with a shell like a woodlouse and millions of feet like a centipede.'

'Sounds horrible,' said Mackey.

'No, he says it's a harmless leaf-eating creature and doesn't bite or sting. That's why it's the emblem of the children's wildlife club. Look, he's done a drawing.'

Joan held up the letter to let them all see.

'What does the wildlife club do?' asked Orla.

'All sorts of things – they're fund-raising for the elephants at the moment.'

'Why do elephants need money?' demanded Mackey.

'They don't, silly. It's to stop poachers killing them. Dara says they need money for more game-wardens and land-rovers and helicopters and things.'

'I saw this awful film on telly last year,' said Orla. 'At least, I saw a bit of it. My Mum turned it off. It was all about elephants being killed by poachers. They showed pictures of dead elephants with their tusks hacked off.' Orla shivered. 'I'm glad my Mum wouldn't let me watch it.'

'That's terrible!' Felicity had been upset at Dara's letter, and Orla's confirmation of the problem only made her feel worse.

'We should do something,' she said.

'Like what?'

'It's too far away. What could we do?'

'We could fund-raise too, and send the money out to Dara.'

'We wouldn't be able to raise much,' said Orla doubtfully.

'Well, it all helps. If everyone sent a little, it would soon be a lot. It's better than doing nothing.'

'Yeah! That's a great idea!' Mackey became all enthusiastic.

'What will we do?' They looked at one another.

'I've got an idea,' said Felicity, who had been thinking about it ever since the letter came. 'We could put on a pageant in the lane – it would be just perfect. We could do Queen Maebh at the Táin Bó Cuailnge – build her a chariot and all.'

'No, I have a better idea,' Mackey said excitedly. 'Romans! Remember that old film *Ben Hur*? It was on telly last summer. It had chariot-racing, with knives strapped to the wheels and all. It was great.'

'That's a bit dangerous,' vetoed Orla sternly. 'We wouldn't be allowed.'

Mackey looked deflated. 'Well, we could do it without the knives, I suppose, but it wouldn't be the same.'

'It would make a super pageant anyway,' declared Jonathan. 'All those costumes, and the chariots racing madly down the lane ....'

'Everyone on the road would want to come and see it,' beamed Muggins.

'Let's do it!' They were all in agreement.

'Right,' said Mackey, taking charge. 'We'll make the chariots, and you girls can do the costumes and the script.'

'That's not fair!' protested Felicity. 'It was my idea. I want to build the chariots.'

'Can't you both build chariots,' said Orla logically, 'if there's going to be more than one?'

☆☆☆

Felicity, restless with enthusiasm, wanted to start her chariot that very afternoon.

'We've got some old pram wheels in our shed,' Orla offered. 'There might be other things there too.'

'I'll come in a few minutes,' said Felicity. 'I want to ask my Mum if I can open our back gates and use the bottom of the garden for building it.'

The Kellys didn't use the back gates. As their house was beside the laneway, they had a more convenient side entrance near the back door. The bottom part of their garden was laid out in vegetables. But behind the vegetables was a big grassy patch which was meant to be the site for a garage – they just hadn't got around to building it yet. But the gates were huge wooden ones, wide enough to drive a car through. They were usually kept locked.

Mrs Kelly's vegetables were a rather sore point with her, which was why Felicity thought she had better ask permission to work near them at all. Her mother wasn't a very good gardener, but she kept thinking that she could supply the house with vegetables if she tried. But so far all her efforts had been failures. Carrots had to be abandoned due to carrot-fly. She put the whole patch in leeks one year, in spite of the fact that nobody in the house really liked leeks. Someone had told her they were easy to grow.

They grew well all right – a bumper crop, in fact. But when they were cooked it was discovered that they were infested with greenfly, right down between the layers. Felicity went around telling everyone that they had boiled greenfly for Sunday dinner, and couldn't understand why her mother didn't see the joke.

Then last year, all the cabbages had been hit by a plague of caterpillars, and the leaves that weren't completely eaten through were covered in a disgusting green slime, so that nobody was willing to even pick them.

This year, it was peas. Rows and rows of stakes were laid out, and string tied along them. The peas were, so far, coming on well, and Mrs Kelly was very pleased with herself. She had five nice rows of lettuces as well, and some scallions.

When Felicity asked if she could open the back gates and use the bottom of the garden for building a chariot, her mother agreed.

'But mind my vegetables,' she warned. 'I don't want anything to happen to them this year.'

'I won't go near them,' promised Felicity.

And so the project started.

Orla brought the pram-wheels out from her shed. They were strong-looking, with silver mudguards. A curved silver handle was welded onto the frame between the wheels.

Felicity stared. There was something very odd about the whole thing.

'How did the pram fit on?'

Orla laughed. 'My Dad sawed off the bits that held the pram, and welded the handle onto the base instead. Remember the time he broke his leg and couldn't drive? It was so my Mum could bring potatoes and heavy stuff from the shops.'

Felicity looked horrified. 'You mean she walked to the village pushing *that*?'

'She had to,' said Orla, 'but she was dead embarrassed. She learned to drive afterwards.'

Orla had brought some useful pieces of wood as well. Felicity got string and nails and a hammer from their own tool-box.

Joan wandered in to have a look, just as Felicity and Orla were figuring out how to tie the wood securely to the pram-frame bottom.

'We should really drill some holes,' Orla said.

Joan appraised their efforts. 'It's going to be too low. You need to build it up higher. Above the level of the mudguards.'

'How do we do that?'

'We've got my old playpen at home. It would make a good platform.'

'Would your Mum mind us using it?'

'Why should she? It's no use any more.'

'Let's bring it here, then.'

They all trailed over to Joan's garden and got the playpen out of the shed. It was a big square one, with wooden bars. They carried it back to Felicity's garden and tried to fit it onto the pram wheels.

'We need something to support it underneath,' mused Orla, 'to stop it pressing on the mudguards ... I know! Just wait.' She ran off up the lane and was back in a few minutes with a large plastic basin.

They put this under the playpen, and shifted things around to find the best position.

'The handle gets in the way a bit.'

'Is that the front or the back?' asked Joan.

'The back, of course,' Felicity said.

Orla laughed. 'But you don't push a chariot.'

'Oh.' Felicity hadn't thought about that. 'Well, it'll have to be the front then.'

They manoeuvred the playpen this way and that, not entirely happy with the way it was sitting.

'It's a bit too big.'

'It'll do, as long as we tie it on securely.'

They spent ages tying it down. Orla found some lovely thick rope in her shed, which was stronger than Felicity's string.

'Right. Let's try it.' They dragged the chariot out into the lane.

'Bags first,' said Felicity. 'You two can pull.'

She climbed into the playpen and held onto the sides.

'Right. Go!'

Orla and Joan heaved and hauled on the pram handle, but nothing happened.

'Pull harder!'

'We can't!'

'There's something sticking.' Orla let go the handle and walked around the chariot, trying to see what was wrong.

'It's the mudguards. They're flat down on the wheels. The basin has gone all squashy, and the playpen is pressing on them.'

Felicity got out and the three of them stood around glumly, considering the problem.

'We could put something else on top of the basin,' Joan suggested.

'That will make the whole thing unsteady. We've got to pull it fast for races. If it's going to wobble all over the place it's no use.'

Orla was nodding her head. 'It's the playpen. It's too big and cumbersome really. We'd be better off doing it the way we were going to in the first place.'

They pulled the chariot back into Felicity's garden, and spent the next half hour untying the dozens of knots they had used to secure the playpen. Finally it was free, and they put it to one side.

They started work again, using the pieces of wood, and tying them to the crossbars of the wheel-frame.

'That's better,' said Orla.

Felicity was undecided. 'But it's not very "chariot" looking. It needs something in front.'

'Wrap a sheet of tinfoil around the handles.'

'That would tear too easily ... I know! A fireguard!'

'A *fireguard*?'

'Yes, it's even curved like the front of a chariot.'

'Brilliant!' said Orla.

'I'll go and get ours. We don't use it in the summer.' Felicity ran off.

She was back in a few minutes with the fireguard from the sitting-room, and they quickly tied it into place. The fireguard was shiny brass, and looked impressive.

'That's it! We've got it now.' Orla clapped her hands.

'Let's try it out again.'

They dragged the chariot out into the lane for the second time. Felicity climbed on, and this time Orla and Joan pulled her along quite easily.

They raced down the lane, whooping and laughing.

'It's super,' yelled Felicity, as they came to a halt by Orla's back gate.

'Let me have a go!'

Felicity climbed off and Joan took her place. Felicity and Orla pulled her back down the lane again.

'Your turn now, Orla.'

Up and down the lane they raced, faster and faster, taking turns. They found that although they had fixed ropes to the handles for reins, in practice, it was necessary for the person riding the chariot to cling to the fireguard for dear life, to avoid being thrown out.

'It works! It's a brilliant chariot!'

They sat in the laneway admiring their handiwork, out of breath after all the running up and down.

'I'd better put the playpen back,' said Joan.

'We'll help.'

They retrieved it from Felicity's garden and set off along the lane. They were just passing Mackey's place when ...

'Geronimo!'

Mackey jumped out of the tree by his back gate, straight into the playpen.

There was a loud crack, as the bottom splintered, and Mackey's feet went clean through. He tottered and grabbed the rails as the girls lost their grip.

'Ouch! Help! My feet! Get me out of here!'

'Stupid boy! It serves you right!'

Mackey stood with his feet jammed through the bottom of the playpen, the splintered wood tearing at his ankles. They had to turn it on its side to get him out.

He sat and rubbed his wounds while the girls returned the playpen to Joan's shed. He was feeling sorry for himself, but got no sympathy.

'What a daft thing to do,' said Orla.

'Lucky for you my Mum doesn't need that any more.'

Mackey hobbled to his feet. 'What were you doing with it anyway?'

'We tried it out for the chariot, but it didn't work.'

'We've got our chariot finished.' Felicity pointed down the lane. 'Do you want to see it?'

They brought Mackey down to Felicity's back gate and showed him the result of their labours.

'It's a bit bokety-looking ... does it work?'

'Have a go and see for yourself.'

Mackey got on and the girls pulled him up and down the lane several times, as fast as they could, turning at such speed that finally he yelled for mercy.

'It's deadly,' agreed Mackey when they let him off at last, 'but there's just one thing wrong.'

'What?'

'You don't have *people* pulling a chariot.'

'Oh ...' They hadn't thought about that one.

'Well, what else can we do?' asked Felicity.

'You need a horse.'

'Don't be stupid. We haven't got a horse.'

'I have,' said Mackey. 'Wait here.'

He came back in a few minutes, dragging Boozer by the collar.

Orla looked at the dog doubtfully. 'Will he be strong enough?'

'Of course he will. The chariot pulls easily.'

'OK then, if you're sure.'

'How do we tie him to it?' Felicity was trying to figure it out, puzzled.

'Rope around his collar?' suggested Joan.

'That'll choke him.'

'I've got the very thing,' said Orla. 'Toddler harness – we have an old one at home. Just wait a sec ....' She ran off down the lane to her own house and was back with it in minutes.

They put Boozer's front paws through the harness and tried to buckle it around him.

'It won't fit – he's too fat.'

'Thread some string through the holes and tie it to the buckle,' suggested Orla.

Mackey knelt down and held Boozer while Felicity tried this.

'OK ... done,' said Felicity. 'It works.'

Nest they attached Boozer to the pram handle by the leather reins.

'Let's try him!'

But Boozer had other ideas.

Normally he was a quiet dog, and didn't exert himself much – unless he happened to catch sight of a cat. He saw one now, ambling in through Felicity's back gate.

Mackey, who was about to climb onto the chariot, was thrown to the ground as Boozer took off after the cat.

In through the gateway he went, and straight into the vegetable garden – his prey zig-zagging madly to avoid him.

When it came to cats, Boozer's speed was phenomenal.

The cat found itself trapped among avenues of staked peas, with hedges on either end. Boozer, completely oblivious to the fact that he was towing a full-sized chariot behind him, ploughed through the peas and lettuces and scallions, this way and

that, back and forward, as the cat frantically tried to find an exit.

'Stop! Stop!' screamed Felicity. 'Mackey, stop him! He's wrecking the garden!'

'Boozer! Boozer! Come here, boy!'

But Boozer was in his element. Some spark of youth was rekindled inside him as he threw himself into his favourite pastime. Soon he was towing not only the chariot, but most of the peas from the garden as well.

The cat finally escaped by jumping the six-foot hedge. Boozer tried to follow; he actually got halfway up the hedge before the weight of the chariot dragged him back and he fell on top of it, where he lay panting – age catching up with him at last.

CHAPTER 14
TROUBLE ALL ROUND

Felicity's mother was furious over the ruined garden – and the mangled fireguard.

Felicity was packed off to bed early, without tea.

Next morning, she awoke to the sound of spadework in the garden. She looked out the window and saw her mother busily digging up the vegetable plot. She quickly got dressed and went downstairs. Jonathan was having his breakfast.

'What's Mum doing?'

'Getting rid of the vegetables ... says she's going to plant grass.'

'Oh,' said Felicity, wondering how to make things all right again.

She went outside, and walked down the garden to her mother. 'Mum, would you like a cup of tea?'

Mrs Kelly stopped, and wiped the perspiration from her face. 'Yes, please. This is thirsty work.' A good night's sleep and an hour's solid digging had got rid of her anger.

'Jonathan and I will dig that if you like,' offered Felicity, hoping to appease her further.

Her mother looked at her with interest. 'Well now, that's the best suggestion I've had yet.'

'I'm really sorry about the vegetables.'

'It doesn't matter,' said Mrs Kelly wearily. 'I don't have the time for them any more.' She gave a rueful look over her ruined garden. 'Pity about the peas, though … they were coming along nicely.'

Felicity went back into the house and made the tea, calling her mother in when it was poured.

Mrs Kelly seemed preoccupied as she sipped her tea.

'I'll tell you what,' she said at last, 'if you get the rest of the gang to help you dig the garden, and leave it ready for sowing grass, I'll give you ten pounds towards your elephant fund.'

'Oh, Mum! I love you!' Felicity threw her arms around her mother.

'On one condition.'

'What's that?'

'No more chariots!'

☆☆☆

Joan was astonished to find her mother in a terrible mood next morning. She had found the broken playpen and acted like it was the end of the world.

'But we don't even need it any more,' protested Joan.

Her mother burst into tears and ran out of the room.

Joan was completely bewildered.

'It's all right,' her granny said gently, putting a comforting arm around her. 'She's just missing your Dad, that's all.' Joan's father wouldn't be back from sea until September. 'Why don't we go down to the shops and buy her a big bunch of flowers? … and give her some time to herself.'

But Mackey was the one in most trouble.

Next morning Boozer couldn't even stand up, and lay whimpering in his basket. Mrs McCarthy, thoroughly alarmed, sent for the vet.

The vet was puzzled – until Mackey admitted to what had happened.

'I'm not surprised,' he said. 'The poor dog is probably covered in bruises. Let's just make sure he hasn't any broken bones, or internal injuries.'

He gave Boozer a thorough examination, and pronounced him as well as could be expected under the circumstances. He left painkillers to make Boozer more comfortable, and said he just needed plenty of rest.

Mackey's mother was furious and packed him off to help his father for a few days, to keep him out of further mischief.

☆☆☆

The gang tried to think of ways to raise more money.

Orla and Jonathan and Muggins went around washing cars, and earned nearly six pounds.

Felicity suggested a White Elephant Sale, which she thought very appropriate. They held it out on the front footpath, selling old comics and toys. It was a great success.

Mackey's father chipped in another fiver for all the work Mackey had done for him, and the grand total reached £26.85. Joan's granny rounded this up to £30.00.

They were very proud of themselves, and sent the money off to Dara to help save the elephants.

CHAPTER 15
GOOSEBERRIES

'Gooseberries!' breathed Mackey. 'Loads of gooseberries. I've never seen so many.'

'That's old Fitzy's garden,' Jonathan warned. 'He's dangerous.'

'He's got a gun,' Muggins said darkly, 'and he shoots anyone who tries to get at his gooseberries.'

'Don't be silly.' Mackey was scathing. 'It's illegal to shoot people.'

There was a short silence as the rest of the gang considered their previous encounters with Mr Fitzhenry. None of them were anxious to tangle with him again.

'You're all chicken!' said Mackey in disgust. 'Afraid to feck a few gooseberries.'

'It's not that,' Jonathan insisted defensively. 'Old Fitzy's really dangerous. He fired his gun at us before, nearly deafened us.'

'Nearly killed us.' Muggins shivered, remembering.

'Blanks!' snorted Mackey.

'What?'

'Blanks. You know, dud shots. Make a lot of noise and smoke to frighten little kiddies.' He grinned, taunting them.

'My Mum says his gun was taken away,' said Joan. 'He didn't have a licence.'

'Well, there you are,' Mackey declared. 'Problem solved. Now when do we go after the gooseberries?'

The gang shifted uncomfortably.

'You don't understand,' Felicity said at last. 'You can never see him coming. He has a hedge halfway up his garden, and he's down to the gooseberries before you even know it.'

'That's easy,' Mackey dismissed the argument with derision. 'We'll post a lookout.'

'Where?'

'Up the Red Belly. You can see the gooseberries and his back door from the very top – I checked.'

'But it's too far to shout,' protested Joan.

'Whistle, silly!' Mackey put on a patient expression. 'Look, somebody keeps watch up the tree. If old Fitzy comes out his back door, they whistle. Then the rest of us have tons of time to escape. Simple.'

It sounded all right. They couldn't argue with Mackey's logic. But they were still undecided.

Mackey forced the issue. 'Right then, what about tomorrow morning? Old Fitzy never gardens until the afternoon.'

'Who'll do lookout?' asked Jonathan reluctantly.

'Well, it has to be someone who can whistle through their fingers.'

'That knocks me out,' said Felicity.

'And me,' sighed Muggins.

'I can,' Orla said doubtfully. 'But it's not very loud.'

'No use.' Mackey dismissed her with a wave of his hand. 'That leaves me and Jonathan and Joan. We'll toss up.'

He took a coin out of his pocket and looked at the other two.

'Heads or tails?'

'Heads,' shouted Joan as the coin spun into the air – and heads it was.

He tossed once more, this time between Joan and himself, and Joan won again.

'You're the lookout,' Mackey declared.

☆☆☆

Next morning they all met in the woods, carrying bags for the gooseberries.

'If anything goes wrong,' advised Mackey, 'head for the Tunnel.'

Joan climbed into position up the Red Belly.

The rest of them headed off in the direction of Mr Fitzhenry's garden, which was near the Tunnel end of the woods.

There was a large ditch running behind the garden which always seemed to have muddy water in the bottom. They jumped the ditch, and stood on the narrow bank up against the wall. The wall was high, and they had to stretch their hands to the top and haul themselves up before they could see into the garden.

'All clear.'

'Wow – just look at the gooseberries!'

'There must be millions and millions.'

'Greedy old man,' said Mackey. 'How can he eat all those himself?'

'Maybe he sells them,' Orla suggested.

'Either way he's a greedy old man. Come on.'

The five of them climbed over the wall in a flash and fanned out among the bushes.

Felicity picked a gooseberry and ate it, her face puckering with the sourness. 'I don't think they're very ripe.'

'Oh, stop complaining,' said Mackey.

'The eaters are all up here,' called Jonathan softly. He had ventured dangerously close to the hedge.

The others followed, and started to fill their bags with plump red gooseberries. Felicity tried another one. It burst sweetly in her mouth. 'Oh, they taste lovely!'

'I know,' said Jonathan happily. He was putting more into his mouth than he was into his bag.

They picked busily for a few minutes. Then came a piercing whistle from the direction of the Red Belly.

'Oh, hell!'

'Run quick! He's coming!'

The gang scattered in confusion, dropping their bags as they ran for the wall.

A glance behind showed the terrifying sight of Mr Fitzhenry bearing down on them with a garden rake held at full length over his head.

'Help! Help!' Mackey wailed as his T-shirt tangled on a gooseberry bush and he yanked desperately to free himself.

The others were over the wall now, and floundering in filthy water, having forgotten about the ditch on the other side.

They clambered out and ran.

Mackey was not so fortunate. He was almost over the wall too, when the garden rake descended on his shoulders with a thump, pinning him firmly.

'Thief! Thief!' screamed Mr Fitzhenry, and tried to rake him downwards.

Mackey, with a superhuman effort born of sheer panic, managed to haul himself free and over the wall – rolling head-first into the ditch.

Mr Fitzhenry was already climbing in pursuit.

Mackey crawled from the ditch, and ran for his life.

☆☆☆

The others were all safe in the Tunnel by the time Mackey arrived. Packed together like sardines, they could hardly move.

'Ssshh! Fitzy's after us!' The gang went very silent.

They could hear a distant clumping, which came nearer and nearer ... then a sound of beating in the undergrowth ... then silence.

They pressed their faces to the ground, hardly daring to breathe.

After a while the clumping started again, this time moving away, until finally it was gone completely.

They stayed there for ages, afraid to move. 'I'm getting sick of hiding squashed up in bushes,' complained Joan.

'You should have stayed up the Red Belly.'

'But I wanted to know what was happening.'

'Go check if Fitzy's gone then,' said Mackey.

'Go yourself!'

'You're the lookout.'

Joan gave him a furious look, but turned and crawled out of the Tunnel. She was back in a couple of minutes.

'All clear.'

They relaxed, and shifted around so they could sit up. This gave everyone a bit more room.

'Mackey! Let's see your back.' Felicity was staring in fascinated horror at Mackey's torn T-shirt. It was black, so stains didn't show, but blood was oozing through the holes.

Felicity lifted up the material gently, and everyone gasped. There were vicious-looking marks all down Mackey's back.

'Old Fitzy caught me with the rake.'

'Pervert!' said Jonathan, outraged. 'He must have sharpened it.'

'You'll have to put something on that quickly,' Orla advised. 'Antiseptic stuff.'

'I'll go and get some,' offered Felicity.

'OK,' said Mackey. 'But I'll have to sneak home for a new T-shirt first. My Ma'll kill me if she sees this one. I won't be long.'

☆☆☆

By the time Felicity arrived back with tubes of cream and plasters, there was still no sign of Mackey. They waited for nearly an hour, before giving up and heading for home themselves.

CHAPTER 16
MAD DOG

That evening, Felicity and Jonathan were having tea when there was a knock on the front door. Their father went to answer it.

They heard him show someone into the sitting-room; after a few minutes he came back to call Mrs Kelly. 'It's a policeman. He wants to talk to both of us.'

Their mother was alarmed. 'Not again! What have you two been up to now?' She glanced at Felicity and Jonathan suspiciously.

'It's OK,' said Mr Kelly. 'He just wants to see us for a minute.'

They went out and closed the door.

Felicity glared at Jonathan. 'Don't you dare disappear!'

Jonathan looked offended. 'I'm not going anywhere.'

They sat in silence until their father came back again, this time to bring them in to see the policeman. He was a different one from the last time – Felicity was relieved. He was small and kind-looking. He introduced himself as Guard O'Leary.

Their parents seemed anxious. 'Why didn't you tell us about Ignatius?' asked Mr Kelly.

Felicity and Jonathan said nothing. Tell what? They needed clues.

'He was attacked by a mad dog,' explained the policeman. 'He says you were there too. I don't mean to upset you, but ... we need a description of the dog,' he ended gently.

Felicity and Jonathan didn't know where to look, or what to say. That stupid Mackey! What had possessed him to think up such a story?'

'We didn't see it,' said Jonathan finally.

The policeman seemed disappointed. 'Nobody seems to have seen it. Funny. It must have been a big one, too, judging by the claw marks on young Ignatius's back.'

Jonathan choked, then started to cough and couldn't stop. His mother had to fetch him a glass of water.

'Look,' said Guard O'Leary, 'I won't delay you any longer. We'll have to find the dog, of course – it's dangerous. Until we do, all youngsters are to stay indoors, and adults too as far as possible. I'll let you know when I have further news.'

He shook hands with them all, and Mr Kelly showed him to the door.

☆☆☆

'Three days! Three whole days!' wailed Joan.

The gang was not amused.

'Whatever possessed you,' asked Orla, 'to say a thing like that?

'My Ma caught me changing my T-shirt and it was the first thing that came into my head. I couldn't tell her what really happened, now could I?'

'You didn't have to involve the rest of us.'

'Well,' said Mackey defensively, 'I didn't know she'd make such a stupid fuss about it. I had to go to hospital for an injection and all ...' He looked rather put-out.

But they were very angry indeed; and three days stuck indoors, restless and bored, made them rather unforgiving. It was a while before good relations were restored.

The fact that they were restored at all was due to something that happened a few days later.

CHAPTER 17
MACKEY'S PROBLEM

'Mackey's crying,' reported Joan. 'He's up the Red Belly and he's crying.'

'What's wrong?' asked Jonathan.

'I don't know. He told me to get lost.'

The gang looked guiltily at one another. They hadn't been very nice to Mackey since the business of the Mad Dog, but they hadn't realised he was that upset.

'Someone better go and talk to him,' Orla said.

'I'll go,' offered Jonathan.

'Better still, see if he'll come down. We'll wait here at the Captain's Table. Tell Mackey we want to say sorry.'

It was ages before Jonathan reappeared, with Mackey in tow. They sat down on the tree-trunk.

Mackey was very subdued.

'I told him we're sorry,' said Jonathan, 'but it's not that ...'

He waited for Mackey to explain.

Mackey seemed reluctant to talk at first. Then it all became too much for him. 'It's my Ma and Da,' he burst out. 'They've split up.'

'Oh, Mackey!' Felicity was appalled. 'That's terrible.'

'No wonder you're upset.'

'Poor Mackey – what a rotten deal!' Orla looked at him, full of sympathy. 'When did they tell you?'

'Yesterday. At least, my Ma told me last night, but my Da was meant to, only he didn't.' Mackey sniffed, and wiped his nose on his sleeve. 'I was spending the day with my Da. He had his afternoon off in the pub, and we were supposed to be going somewhere, only we didn't go anywhere ... and he was in a terrible humour. So I just sat in the pub and talked to some of the fellas I know. Then it was tea-time, and my Da called me, and he went to hang up my jacket and got it upside down and all the cigarette butts fell out. He nearly went berserk ... screamed and roared at me and called me all kinds of things. So I grabbed my jacket and ran, and got the bus home. My Ma was hopping mad when she heard, and she told me herself.'

'Well then,' Felicity consoled, 'maybe it's only a quarrel. Maybe they'll make it up again.'

'They've known all along,' said Mackey bitterly. 'Ever since we came here. That's why my Ma moved out. All that guff about wanting a better life for me – it was lies ...all lies.'

'I'm sure that part wasn't lies.' Orla spoke gently. 'It is better for you here, isn't it?'

Mackey kicked at the tree trunk, but didn't answer.

'Maybe when he comes out to see you, you could talk to them both – try to get them back together again,' suggested Felicity.

'He never comes, never! He hasn't come since we moved, not once. He always says he's too busy. He hasn't even seen the house!'

The gang were silent. What could they say?

'There must be something you could do,' said Muggins brightly.

'What?'

'I don't know.' Muggins looked crestfallen.

'Everybody think,' Orla ordered.

They all thought as hard as they could, but no ideas came.

'It doesn't mean that they don't love you,' ventured Felicity.

Mackey rounded on her with a terrible look on his face. 'I've had all that rubbish from my Ma already,' he screamed. 'So shut it! I don't want to hear!'

The rawness of his emotion frightened them. There was a dimension to Mackey's anger that they didn't, and couldn't, understand.

Felicity was hurt that he could talk to her like that. She was only trying to help.

There was an uncomfortable silence. No one else offered suggestions – they were afraid to, now.

Finally Mackey got up. 'I'm going home.'

He turned and went off through the woods. The gang stared helplessly after him.

CHAPTER 18
TROUBLE AGAIN!

Next morning Felicity found herself alone in the woods. No one else wanted to come out; Mackey's news had put a damper on things.

She decided she might as well go and practise climbing the Red Belly, although it was hard to work up any enthusiasm for the task. 'I'll never climb this tree,' she thought in despair, looking up at the big branch way above her head.

She searched around the base of the trunk for a starting point, and found a tiny knob a foot or so above the ground. She stood on this with one foot, grasping the trunk tightly between her hands, and felt around with her other foot for a second hold. Then, balancing on the tips of her toes, face pressed tight against the tree, she gingerly released her right hand to feel upwards for a finger hold. Over to one side, then the other. Up a bit higher, and higher ... there! Stretching as far as she could, Felicity found a tiny, but deep, crack. Once her index-finger was jammed in, she was secure enough to try for a higher foot-hold. Finding one, she hauled herself upwards. With her left hand, she now felt across the trunk for another hand-hold ... nothing. Then she stretched as far as she could around the back – nothing again.

She tried for ages, but couldn't seem to progress further. Exhausted, she rested for a moment, spreadeagled against the tree, cheek to cheek with its rough bark.

'Gotcha!'

There was a triumphant shout from below, and a pair of arms clamped around her legs, nearly dislodging her.

'Let go!' she screamed. 'I'll fall!' She couldn't see who the culprit was.

There was a loud chuckle and the arms clamped even tighter, until one foot slipped, and Felicity felt herself falling backwards. She landed on something soft, and rolled over.

Harold was lying there beside her, a look of surprise on his face. He had taken Felicity's full weight and was a bit winded.

Felicity sat up, feeling something odd crunch beneath her as she did. She moved over to see what it was.

'I got glasses yesterday,' said Harold sadly. 'That's why I fell in the lake – I couldn't see properly.'

The gold wire frames were all squashed, and one circle of glass had fallen out completely. At least that wasn't broken, which was something.

Felicity looked at the spectacles in desperation. She'd be blamed for this – she was always blamed. 'Maybe we can fix them,' she said.

She picked them up and tried to straighten the frame, but it was stronger than it appeared.

She tried to put the circle of glass back. It would only go three-quarters of the way in. 'We need a pliers,' she decided, 'and some sellotape.'

Harold looked at her admiringly.

'Wait here, I'll be back in a few minutes.' Felicity ran off home to see what she could find in the toolbox. She returned with pliers, sellotape and a piece of thin wire, and set to work.

It was harder than she had expected.

Every time she straightened one bit of the frame, it made another bit bend. The glass wouldn't go in completely, either, in spite of her best efforts to stretch the frame, so she taped it carefully on with sellotape. One of the arms was hanging loose at the hinge; she carefully fixed it with some of the wire.

Finally, she got Harold to try them on. 'Can you see all right?'

'Yes.'

'Good.' She sighed with relief. The glasses looked OK. Maybe no one would notice.

They walked back up the lane together, Felicity having decided that she'd done enough climbing for one day.

✩✩✩

'I really don't know what gets into you, Felicity,' scolded Mrs Kelly in exasperation. 'It's just one thing after another.'

'It wasn't my fault!'

'It never is. But it costs me money just the same.'

'And me,' said Felicity bitterly. No pocket money for a month – and she'd only just got it back again after the business at the lake. 'It's not fair! I didn't do anything!'

'I agree, it's *not* fair. I have to pay half the cost of new glasses, and I didn't do anything either.'

'It was all Harold's fault.'

Her mother sighed. 'Look, Felicity, perhaps it was Harold's fault in the first place, but if you had sent him home with his glasses, everything would have been fine. You just don't stop to think. Once you got at them with the pliers, they were a complete write-off.'

'I was only trying to help.'

Her mother sighed again. 'I know ... but the responsibility is yours just the same.'

Responsibility. Felicity hated that word.

CHAPTER 19
THE IDEA

'I've got it!' said Orla. 'I've got it.'

'Got what?'

The gang were all sitting around the Captain's Table, pondering their difficulties.

'The solution to all our problems.'

'Tell us.'

'We'll have a concert!'

'You're joking.' No one was impressed. They weren't much in the mood for concerts.

'No, really. Just listen. Let me explain.' Orla had been thinking it through for some time. 'Mackey wants to get his dad out here – right?'

'Right,' said Mackey glumly.

'Well then, we could plan a really good concert, with a play and all. Then Mackey could invite his dad to come and see it.'

There was silence as they all digested the idea – but Mackey's face was no longer glum. Orla had just handed him a lifeline.

'My Da always comes to school concerts,' he said excitedly. 'He never misses them.'

'Well, then?'

'He'll come. He'll come! He can't refuse to come and see me in a play, can he?' Mackey was half talking to himself. He grinned, and thumped Orla on the back in appreciation.

Suddenly they were all talking at the same time, relieved that the strain was over.

Orla held up her hand and shouted, 'Just a minute! That's not all.'

She got immediate attention.

'We can solve two problems at once.'

'Two?' The others were puzzled.

'As well as making Mackey's dad come here, it can be a benefit concert for Felicity. We'll charge all the adults in.'

They stared at Orla, lost in admiration.

Mackey was particularly enthusiastic. 'Hey, that's deadly, that is.' He had secretly felt just a little bit bad about Felicity losing her pocket money over his antics at the lake.

Felicity wasn't arguing either.

'We'll have to make a plan,' said Orla.

They started discussing what they might do.

'Let's have a pirate play,' suggested Mackey. 'I've got some great ideas.'

'And I want to do a ballet dance. I know a brilliant one.' Orla started to pirouette around on her tippy-toes. 'It's called the Dance of the Seven Veils.' Orla had been fascinated by the name for years, ever since she'd read it in a book.

Mackey started to laugh. 'That I've got to see!'

'What's so funny?'

Mackey kept laughing, and refused to share the joke. Orla got quite offended.

'Order! Order!' shouted Jonathan. 'We'd better make out a list. I'll go and get the logbook from the Red Belly.'

They were waiting for Jonathan to come back, when a voice piped up from behind Felicity. 'Can I be in the concert too?'

It was Harold.

'Go away,' said Felicity. 'You're nothing but trouble – and a tell-tale too.'

'I didn't tell.'

'You did so.'

'I didn't. Honest I didn't.' Harold looked upset. 'Mrs Finnerty saw us coming up the lane and you had the pliers and things, so she told my mother. She thought we were up to mischief.'

Felicity softened. 'OK. I'm sorry I called you a tell-tale.'

'Can I be in your gang?'

'No. You're too young.'

'I'm not!'

'You are.'

'I am *not*.' Harold stared at her stubbornly.

'Look, why don't you start your own gang, with your own friends – then you could even be the leader.'

Harold considered the suggestion carefully. 'I never thought of that.'

'Well, get lost and think about it,' said Mackey rudely.

But Harold wasn't finished yet. 'Where can I have my gang?'

'Oh, anywhere you like, for heaven's sake,' Joan snapped, exasperated.

'OK. I'll have it here.'

'Look what you did now, stupid.' Mackey glared accusingly at Joan.

'Don't call me stupid!'

'Hold on! Hold on!' Felicity turned to Harold. 'Now, Harold,' she said in a reasonable tone. 'This is our place. Can't you have your gang somewhere else?'

'Where?'

'You've got a great garden shed.'

Harold thought about this, and grudgingly admitted it might make a headquarters. 'But we'll still need somewhere to climb.'

'Well, you can't climb here,' declared Muggins. The gang were getting thoroughly fed up.

Harold delivered his trump card.

'Why not? You don't own the woods.'

There was a terrible silence, during which Jonathan returned with the logbook.

'Harold,' said Felicity slowly, 'will you go away until we call you? We have to discuss this among ourselves.'

When Harold was gone, Felicity turned to the others.

'He's right. We don't ... you know ... own the woods.'

'What's going on?' asked Jonathan, bewildered.

They quickly filled him in on what had taken place in his absence.

Orla was frowning. 'We may have to do a deal.'

'What kind of deal?' Jonathan wasn't one bit pleased.

'Offer him some of our territory.'

'Give him the Tunnel,' suggested Muggins. 'We're getting too big for it anyway.'

'No good. He won't agree to that. It's climbing-trees he's after.'

They thought about it for a few minutes.

'I'll tell you what,' said Felicity at last. 'When I learn to climb the Red Belly, he could have the Captain's Table, and the trees around it. As long as he promised to keep away from our other places.'

'He's not getting the Captain's Table!' They were outraged.

'Just the trees, so.'

'Then it won't be private here any longer.'

'Where else? If we don't give him something good he'll only pester us.'

'She's right,' agreed Orla.

'It might never come to that anyway.' Jonathan brightened up a bit. 'Felicity won't be up the Red Belly for at least another year. Maybe Harold will have forgotten all about it by then.'

They had to agree. It was the only solution they could think of for the moment.

Harold agreed, too, when they called him back. 'OK,' he said, pleased with the arrangement.

'Now buzz off,' said Mackey with feeling.

Harold smiled.

'But can I just be in your concert first ....'

'No!'

'No way.'

'Then I promise I'll go away and make my own gang.'

'Get lost.' Jonathan glared at him.

'Please?'

'No!'

'Just this once?'

'*No!*'

'Oh, let him,' said Felicity, suddenly realising that they were never going to get rid of Harold.

There was a pause.

'Well,' Mackey conceded grudgingly, 'I suppose you could be a pirate.'

'I want to play my violin.'

'Suffering ducks. The bloody violin! That's all we need.' Mackey grimaced in disgust.

'You've got no culture,' said Orla, still a bit miffed over Mackey laughing at her Dance of the Seven Veils. 'His violin will go very well with my ballet. And besides, the adults will love it. Now, anyone else want to perform?'

No one did.

'That's settled then. All we have to do now is write the play.'

They set to work that very day.

'Treasure Island,' insisted Mackey. 'I fancy being Long John Silver.' He stiffened one leg and went clumping about in a very funny way, holding a fist to one shoulder for the parrot, and squawking so loudly that they all had to stick their fingers in their ears.

When they had stopped laughing, Jonathan said, 'That's great. And I'll be Captain Hook.'

'Captain Hook's not from Treasure Island,' Joan pointed out.

'Who cares? We can do it any way we like.'

'Right, then,' Mackey said, 'the rest of you can be ordinary pirates.'

'That's not fair,' protested Felicity. 'I don't want to be an ordinary pirate. I wanted to be Captain Hook too. We should have auditions.'

'A girl can't be Captain Hook.'

'Why not?'

'Because girls aren't pirates, that's why.'

'What about Granuaile?'

'Who's she?'

'Didn't they teach you any history at your school?' demanded Orla. 'Granuaile was the Pirate Queen of Ireland. She sailed all around the coast robbing people and castles and things. Everyone was terrified of her. She was fiercer than any man.'

'OK then, Felicity can be Granuaile.'

'I don't want to be Granuaile. You be Granuaile!' Felicity looked crossly at Mackey.

'Don't be silly,' said Mackey. 'A fella can't play a girl pirate.'

'Why not? They do it in pantomimes all the time – like the ugly sisters.'

'That's different.'

'What's different about it?'

'Look,' said Orla desperately, 'I'll be Granuaile. Think of another pirate name for Felicity.'

'Bluebeard?'

Felicity reluctantly agreed. It didn't have quite the scope of Captain Hook, but at least he was an important pirate too.

'And what about me?' asked Muggins. 'Can I be Captain Flint?'

They all laughed and Muggins became quite annoyed. 'What's so funny?'

'Captain Flint is the parrot, sillyboots,' said Mackey.

'Oh.' Muggins was downcast.

'I don't mind. You can be Captain Flint if you think you can sit on my shoulder.' Mackey went into cackles of laughter again.

'Stop it, Mackey.' Orla felt sorry for her brother. 'The parrot was called after a real Captain Flint, in case you didn't know. Muggins can be Captain Flint if he wants.'

'But the story won't be right then.'

'It doesn't have to be. With Captain Hook and Granuaile, it's not going to be Treasure Island anyway.'

Nobody noticed that Joan had been keeping very quiet. Now she spoke up. 'Who said it had to be a pirate play anyway? I don't remember voting.'

They all looked at her in surprise.

'But a pirate play is best,' said Mackey.

'Why?'

'It just is – all swordfights and walking the plank and things – action.'

'I think it's disgusting. There's enough violence in the world already.'

There was an embarrassed silence.

'OK. What do you want to do?'

'Something not violent – like Peter Pan and Wendy ...'

'That's Captain Hook. Peter Pan is full of pirates.'

'... without the violent bits,' finished Joan.

'But that's all the good bits!'

'No it's not. What about the time they learned how to fly? And Wendy sewing Peter's shadow back on? And Tinkerbell getting stuck in the drawer?'

'We can't make a play out of that!'

'Why not? Or something else then, like Cinderella?'

Mackey groaned, 'I don't believe this.'

'We'd better have a vote,' said Jonathan, who was keeping track of things in the logbook. 'All those in favour of a pirate play, put your hands up.'

Everyone's hand went up except Joan's.

'Sorry. Outvoted on that one.'

Joan got to her feet. 'Well, I'm not going to be in any silly pirate play. And that's that!'

'Ah Joan.'

'Please.'

'Don't spoil things.'

'I'm not the one who's spoiling things.' Joan gave Mackey a hateful look.

'Well, the fact is the rest of us like the idea,' Orla said slowly, 'and you're supposed to agree to whatever wins a vote.'

Joan didn't say anything for a minute. She knew she was being put on the spot. While she was determined not to give in to Mackey and his stupid pirate play, she knew that the vote had been fairly won. Unwilling to lose face by backing down, she had a sudden inspiration.

'I'll do the door. Somebody will have to collect money, and get everyone seated.'

'We never thought of that.'

'Right, so. Joan's on the door, and the rest of us are pirates. If we include Harold, that will make six again.' Jonathan wrote it carefully down in the logbook.

'Now, most important. Where will we have the play?'

'We could use our garage,' said Orla, 'but we'd have to clear it out. It's stuffed with junk.'

They were delighted with that. The Duggans' garage was absolutely enormous.

'How do we make a stage?'

'We don't,' Mackey explained. 'We just rope off a section of the garage and decorate it like a ship. We can tie a long piece of wood over boxes for walking the plank.' He grinned wickedly in anticipation.

'I'll have to find something to dance on,' said Orla. 'The concrete will tear my ballet shoes.'

'Polish it.'

'Or put that chalk stuff down.'

'No, it's too rough. I'll ask my Mum.'

'We'll have to have a box for Harold to stand on when he plays his violin, or else he won't be seen.'

Jonathan was busy making notes. 'Anything else?'

'Who's going to do the costumes?' asked Felicity warily.

'We'll each do our own,' suggested Orla, 'whatever way we like.'

'OK. What about knives, then?' Jonathan waited, biro poised.

'Real knives are out.'

'I've got one of those great joke knives that goes down into the handle when you stab someone,' said Mackey. 'It's only plastic, but it looks real. We could buy some more.'

'And we've got those wooden strips in our garage,' Muggins broke in. 'They'd be great for swords.'

'Brilliant!' Jonathan entered it all down in the logbook.

'We need a copybook for writing the play.'

'Who wants to write?'

'We'll all help. Everyone pool ideas.'

'I have a deadly idea for an ending,' said Mackey. 'A really gory one that will have everyone screaming.'

Joan got up. 'I'm going home for tea.' She marched out.

'She really doesn't like the pirate play,' Orla said worriedly.

'Well, the rest of us do.' Mackey was quite firm. 'She needn't write it, or come to rehearsals or anything ... just turn up on the day and do the door. She doesn't even have to watch it, if it comes to that.'

'I suppose so.'

'Right then,' Jonathan said, 'about the plot ... '

CHAPTER 21
PREPARATIONS

A week before the concert, they started to clear out the Duggans' garage. Mrs Duggan insisted that they clear it completely. She didn't want things like oil and garden shears lying around, or anything that might possibly injure anyone ... or anything that anyone might trip over.

It was a huge job.

Joan missed all the work, as she went to stay with her auntie in Wexford for a week.

They carted out the cans of paint and stored them in Mackey's shed. Lawnmowers, shears, spades and forks went into the Duggans' boiler-house. Bicycles were left outside, against the garage wall. An old wardrobe had to be dragged into the garden and put lying on its face in case it fell on anyone. Fishing tackle was removed, temporarily, to Mr Duggan's bedroom. Pram wheels and a large baby-bath were left at the back of Felicity and Jonathan's garden, along with a broken kitchen chair.

'Mum says there's a roll of lino that I can use for dancing on.'

'We haven't found any lino.'

'Well, it's here somewhere.'

'We've loads to shift yet,' said Jonathan. 'Look at all those newspapers – they must go back donkey's years.'

Down one end, the stacks of newspapers nearly reached the ceiling.

'Couldn't we use them for extra seating?' suggested Felicity. 'We only have two benches so far.'

'Hey, that's a great idea! Tie them into piles and push them together.'

'They're tied in piles already, but the piles aren't even.'

'Leave them until the last – we've to sweep the place out properly first.'

'Where will I put this?' Mackey hauled out a huge case he'd found in a corner.

'What's in it?'

'I dunno.'

'Open it,' said Muggins.

The case wasn't locked, and proved to be full of old curtains – plain ones, patterned ones, both long and short. There were nets too, yellow with age.

'Hey, we can use this stuff.'

'My Mum hates throwing anything out,' said Orla. 'I'll ask her if we can borrow them.'

'Look,' called Mackey. 'There's another case here – a big trunk. Give us a hand.'

Muggins ran to help, and they pulled the trunk out from under a pile of old carpets. It was a brown trunk with pale wooden battens and metal studs all over it.

'Treasure!' shouted Mackey. ' Pieces of eight.' He staggered around the garage doing his Long John Silver impression, making them all laugh.

'I'm sure it's not filled with pieces of eight,' said Orla, 'but we can make use of the trunk as a stage prop.'

The trunk was filled with old clothes and belts, which would be useful for costumes, or to provide material to make things.

'Can I help too?' Harold had come into the garage without any of them noticing.

'OK.'

They were getting used to Harold, as he had already attended rehearsals for the play. Felicity couldn't get over the change in him – the way he never threw tantrums any more. He didn't really have a part, other than to run around looking fierce. But he was more than pleased with that. He was doing his own violin practice at home by agreement. Mackey declared once was enough to listen to that stuff.

'My cousins are coming to the concert,' announced Harold. 'With my three aunties, and my uncles, and my granny and grandad too.'

They all stopped and stared at him.

'How may people is that?'

Harold had to calculate hard for a few moments, counting on his fingers. 'Thirteen, I think.'

'That's an unlucky number.'

'Well, my Mum and Dad make two more.'

'Wow!'

They looked at him in amazement.

Orla sat down on the trunk. 'You know what this means?' she said faintly.

'What?'

'We'll have to be good. Put on a really professional show. It's one thing having just our parents, and brothers and sisters, and kids on the road ... but all those people! They'll be expecting something great.'

'I thought the idea was to be great anyway,' said Felicity.

'I know. But we mightn't be. Things can go wrong.'

'Does it matter?'

'Yes it does – if we're going to charge money in to the public.'

'They won't care,' Mackey declared. 'They know it's just us.'

'I told them we were really good,' said Harold proudly.

That had them all worried. They continued to clear out the garage, thinking hard.

'I know,' said Felicity suddenly. 'Dress rehearsal.'

'Dress rehearsal?'

'Yes. If we have a dress rehearsal on Saturday, and the performance proper on Sunday, then we'll know what sort of things can go wrong, and have time to fix them.'

'Yeah. All the proper theatres do that,' Mackey said.

'We can invite the kids on the road to the Saturday show,' continued Felicity, 'and leave Sunday free for visitors and adults.'

'That's it!'

'Brilliant!'

The idea was greeted with approval all round.

'Will we charge in to the dress rehearsal?'

'Yes. Something small. It's not the same if it's free,' decided Orla.

'And I've just thought of another idea,' said Felicity with mounting excitement. 'We can use really good seats on the Sunday. We've got six patio chairs with cushions. I could bring them along.'

'We have padded kitchen chairs,' chipped in Orla.

'So have we,' said Mackey.

'We could do the place up really nice,' Felicity added, 'and maybe even give everyone a cup of tea afterwards. Than people would feel they had got their money's worth.'

'I knew it was going to be great,' said Harold, looking at Felicity with pride. 'I told them so.'

Orla had gone all thoughtful. 'We're a bit thin on the concert end though – do you think they'll mind?'

'What do you mean?'

'Well, only two acts. We've got dancing, and an instrument. We could do with a third act as well – something different ... a singer, say.'

'I can't sing a note,' said Muggins with satisfaction.

'Jonathan?'

'No jolly fear!' He hated his beautiful soprano voice.

'Joan's granny sings all the time,' offered Felicity.

'So does my dog,' joked Mackey.

'What?'

'Does he really?' Orla looked interested.

'Well, I used to do "How Much is that Doggie in the Window?" with him, and he could bark at all the right bits. But I haven't tried it for ages. He used to howl at the "1812 Overture" too. My Da has the record and he had to stop playing it.'

'Could he still do it?' demanded Orla.

'I don't know. I suppose so.'

'Then find out! It's just what we need – a novelty act. "Boozer the Singing Dog" – just perfect. Imagine that on the posters!'

CHAPTER 22
THE PLAY

The day of the dress rehearsal dawned bright and clear.

None of them could eat much breakfast, discovering, to their surprise, that they had butterflies in their tummies. There was nothing to be nervous about, but their bodies reacted like that all the same.

Mrs Kelly laughed at the half-finished bowls of cornflakes.

'I'm just a bit excited,' said Felicity.

'It's stage-nerves. You know, even famous actors and actresses feel like that before every performance.'

'Do they really?' asked Jonathan, who felt so awful he thought he might be coming down with the flu.

'Yes. It's quite normal,' confirmed their father cheerfully, tucking into a plate of bacon and eggs. 'I remember a part I had in a school play once. It went on for a whole week, and I vomited up every meal I ate.'

'Please, John!' Mrs Kelly protested. 'Not at the table.'

But it made Felicity and Jonathan laugh, and they felt a bit better.

The performance was to start at 3:00 p.m., but all the props had to be re-checked before that, for safety.

The stage looked magnificent. They had painted the decks of a pirate ship onto old sheets as a back-drop. A white skull and crossbones had been stuck on a black pillowcase as the Jolly Roger, and this lay at the bottom of its flagpole waiting to be raised at the start of the play. An eight-foot length of chipboard, which they'd found in the garage, made a super plank when tied to the end of an old kitchen table. The plank was supported underneath by a solid bank of newspapers, and stretched down into the centre isle, with seats for the audience on either side of it. It was important to make sure the plank was secure, as it had to stand up to quite a bit of use during the play. But they all tested it by jumping up and down and running back and forward along its length, and it proved solid as a rock. Behind the table, bales of newspaper formed steps leading up to the plank.

Large wooden boxes had been piled together to form the wheelhouse of a ship, and sheets had been hung up for sails. Lengths of rope were strung around, and coiled on the deck. The old trunk made an impressive treasure chest. All the curtains came in handy to make 'wings' at each side of the garage. Two corners were curtained off completely, so that only the characters who were meant to be on stage could be seen.

The costumes had been great fun to put together.

Mackey, as Long John Silver, had a man's jacket with gold braid sewn all along its edges. He wrapped his leg to the knee in brown elastic bandage for a peg-leg, and kept it completely stiff.

An upside-down sweeping brush made a perfect crutch when the handle was cut down a bit.

Mackey had originally intended to double up his own leg inside his trousers, and use a proper piece of wood as a false leg. But this posed problems of mobility as it was nearly impossible to move around, let alone fight, with that arrangement – and he couldn't walk for ages afterwards as it gave him a cramp.

Jonathan chose an oversized white shirt, tucked into a pair of black leggings, with a wide leather belt and a bandanna round his head. He had made his hooked hand himself, and was very proud of the result.

Orla had some difficulty trying to decide what looked grand enough for Granuaile. The problem was solved by the discovery of a purple velvet curtain in the case, which made a fine cloak. She wore her black leotard and tights underneath, with a thick leather belt to hold her sword and knife. This gave her little changing to do after her ballet dance. She decided not to wear anything on her head, but scrunched her hair up with gel to look suitably wild, and let it hang all over her face.

Felicity made a magnificent beard out of a thick wad of cotton-wool, which she dyed black. It actually turned out bluey-black, which didn't really matter. She attached it to a pirate's hat which she had made. Only the centre of her face was visible when it was in place, and this she rubbed with soot to make her look fierce. An old jacket and trousers, with a long red sash around her waist, completed the picture.

Muggins, who insisted on keeping the name of Captain Flint, picked a red shirt, a leather jerkin, and baggy trousers, with a multicoloured scarf for around his head. He made a black patch to go over one eye.

Harold's mother sewed a costume, as she didn't want him dressing up in dirty old clothes.

Joan was back from her holidays. She had missed the rehearsals and was quite looking forward to seeing the play, in spite of what she had said. She set up a kitchen table near the garage door for collecting money. It was decided to keep the big car-doors of the garage closed, as they would let in too much light and spoil the atmosphere. There was a small side door for people to come in and out without having to open the main doors. So this was where she put the table.

They had all collaborated on the poster for outside:

GRAND BENEFIT CONCERT
Dance of the Seven Veils – By Orla

Harold on Violin

Boozer – The Sensational Singing Dog

☆☆☆

And featuring play of the season –

Gala Premiere of

'Blood and Guts on Treasure Island'

☆☆☆

Plenty of Action (Fights etc.)

Come along and enjoy, and support a good cause.

Saturday 3.00 pm .... Children Only 10p

Sunday 3.00 pm .... Adults 30p

Orla thought the blood and guts bit was a little too strong, but the boys overruled her, and Felicity quite liked it too.

Mr Duggan photocopied the poster for them at his office, and they posted copies through all the letter-boxes on Conker Road.

So, with everything set up and ready, and double-checked, they waited impatiently as the clock ticked slowly, ever so slowly, around towards three o'clock.

CHAPTER 23
ACTION STATIONS!

Orla was on first. This was because of the lino.

They had finally found it beneath the stack of newspapers. It had to be spread out on the floor for the ballet, then taken up again before anyone could trip over the edges.

She was dressed in a black leotard and tights. Seven large, brightly coloured headscarves floated from the belt around her waist, each one knotted by a single corner. It looked like she was wearing a long skirt at first, but when the music was played on the tape recorder, and she started to dance, they flew out around her in all directions. She pirouetted back and forward on her pointes, flowing and graceful. The only thing missing was a spotlight. Orla insisted, at first, that she needed one, but they couldn't figure out how to organise it. So she had to make do with the garage light on, and the windows blacked out – which wasn't quite the same thing, but it was the best they could manage. The audience, with a bit of encouragement from Felicity, clapped enthusiastically at the end.

Then came Harold.

A wooden box was put in the centre of the floor for him to stand on, and he played his piece unaccompanied.

'Hey, he's really good.' Felicity was surprised.

'My Mum says he won medals at the Feis,' said Orla.

Harold seemed quite a different person when he played his violin – more grown-up or something – as he concentrated totally on what he was doing. At the end, he bowed formally to the audience, and they all clapped.

Boozer was on next.

Mackey tried to get him to sit up on Harold's box, but he was having none of it. However, as soon as the tape recorder was turned on, and the strains of Tchaikovsky's '1812 Overture' filled the garage, Boozer started to howl mournfully; and kept on and on and on. It was a bit frightening really – he looked like a wolf, with his head thrown back and his nose up in the air.

'Turn it off, Jonathan,' Mackey hissed. 'He's had enough.'

As soon as the music stopped, Boozer lay down and tried to go to sleep. Mackey hauled him up again, slipping him something nice to eat on the palm of his hand. Boozer chewed contentedly. The tape recorder was turned on again.

'How much is that doggie in the window?' sang Mackey, accompanying the tape he had made earlier in the week.

'Woof-woof!' went Boozer, to the children's absolute delight.

'The one with the waggly tail ...'

'Woof-woof!'

'How much is that doggie in the window?'

'Woof-woof!'

'I do hope that doggie's for sale ...'

'Woof-woof-woof-woof!' Boozer got excited at the children laughing so much. He raced down into the audience and started licking faces all around him, and trying to jump up on laps. There was consternation until Mackey hauled him back up to the stage again to complete the other verses of the song. Boozer was in great form, performing on cue and barking in all the right places. Mackey gave him a big hug when he finished, and the audience went wild, clapping and demanding more, so that Boozer had to do an encore. Mackey brought him home in the short interval before the play started, and left him to snooze in peace in the garden after his virtuoso performance.

☆☆☆

It was time for the play.

The garage was plunged into pitch darkness for a minute, and when the light came on again there were three pirates on stage: Captain Hook in the centre, Granuaile standing dramatically on the top deck behind him, and pirate Harold on duty by the flagpole.

Jonathan stepped forward.

'Heigh-ho! Avast! I'm Captain Hook,
A terrifying pirate crook.
I fight my way around the world
With Jolly Roger flag unfurled ...'

At a signal, Harold pulled on the rope which raised the Jolly Roger to the top of the flagpole.

All the children cheered, and Jonathan continued:

'Now everyone's afraid of me

Because of this strange hook you see
That I have growing as a hand –
Now those who want a look, please stand!'

There was a pause to let the message sink in, then one by one, the children stood up, until nobody at all was left sitting. Jonathan went in among the audience, with much heigh-ho-ing and avast-me-heartying, prodding and poking at them with his hook. He was very proud of this hook, which was made out of a length of hanger wire pushed through a round piece of wood and bent in a wide semi-circle. There was a piece of elastic stapled to the other side of the wood for his fingers to go through, and the sleeve of his shirt had been pinned around the wood to make it really secure.

'It's only pretend,' said one little boy loudly.

Jonathan swung around with a snarl and hooked the boy by the neck, pulling him close. 'You said something, me hearty?'

'No! No!' The boy began to bawl.

'For heaven's sake, Jonathan,' called Felicity from the wings, 'You're frightening the children!'

Jonathan swung fiercely around to the audience. 'Is anyone afraid?' he roared.

'No! No! No!' they roared back, terrified.

Jonathan grinned his most devilish grin, which was quite awful as he had blackened out a few of his teeth. He stalked flamboyantly back onto the stage, where Orla was waiting to be introduced, and declared:

'Oh, piracy! My Love! My Life!
And now, me hearties, here's the wife ...'

'Keep to the script,' hissed Orla furiously. She had to think quickly now, to get out of this one.

'He jokes! He jokes! I'm not his wife.
Who'd want to live with him for life?
I'm much too busy pirating,
For I'm a famous Pirate Queen –
I'm Granuaile! I'm Granuaile!
And at my name the strongest quail!'

She swung her cloak around with a flourish and glowered at the children through her shaggy curtain of hair.

'I capture castles by the score,
And villages along the shore.
I am the terror of the sea
And everyone's afraid of me.
North, south, and east and west I sail,
I'm Granuaile! I'm Granuaile!'

Her voice rose at the end of a high wailing note.

Harold, meanwhile, having performed his duty of raising the Jolly Roger, was busy trying out his sword – slashing it furiously into thin air. Orla frowned at him as she finished her speech, and he stopped, putting the sword away in his belt.

Jonathan spoke again.

'And now, me hearties, let us go
To find the enemy pirates, so
That we can steal their treasure map
And ships and gold and things like that.'

He stopped for a minute, then warned the audience in a snarling voice:

'Old Long John Silver hides somewhere,
If you should see him, do take care.
And do not say you saw me here
Or – I – will – split – you – ear – to – ear!'

Jonathan produced his dagger and bared his blackened teeth at them, looking very fierce

154

indeed. He drew the dagger slowly across his neck to emphasise the point. The audience were deathly silent as Captain Hook and Granuaile and Harold slipped away to one side of the stage...

Enter Long John Silver, and Bluebeard, and Captain Flint.

Felicity looked terrific as Bluebeard. Nobody would have recognised her. The beard reached down to her knees and covered half her face. Mackey was in his element as Long John Silver, clumping around the place. He'd even managed to find a parrot. One of the customers in the pub had given him a toy parrot on a swing when he heard about the play, and it was perfect. Mackey had removed the parrot from its swing and pinned it to the shoulder of his jacket.

'Yo-ho-ho, and a bottle of rum!' sang Mackey at the top of his voice, then stopped and faced the audience, sniffing suspiciously.

'Old Hook is somewhere, I can tell.
I smell the critter's pirate smell.
I smell his smell upon the air.
He's somewhere round about – but where?'

'Do – you – know – where?' he roared at the audience, glaring at them fiercely.

The poor children didn't know what to do. The ones in the front rows yelled *'No,'* and the ones safe in the back yelled *'He's in there,'* pointing at the wing.

'A-ha,' said Long John Silver with a knowing look.

'I must consult with my good mates,
This helpful information rates
A lot of caution, I'll be bound –

Our Treasure Map must not be found!'
Felicity now stepped forward.
'I'm Captain Bluebeard and I've got
A treasure map that shows the spot
Where treasure lies, where treasure lies,
Just look at this, and feast your eyes!'

She reached inside her jacket and, with a flourish, pulled out a rolled-up map. She opened it up and held it out at arm's length towards the audience, so they could see the big red X marked on it.

'We're very clever pirates, see?

I'm sure you people will agree ...' She glared at the audience and roared: *'Well? ... Agree! Agree! Shout "Yes"!'*

'Yes! Yes! Yes!' yelled the children, getting into the mood of things, now they knew what was expected of them. They gasped, as a figure in a purple cloak darted out from the wings, speared the map with a sword, and was gone again.

Muggins sent up a loud wailing.
'Alas! Alas! Our treasure's gone.
Our treasure's gone. Our treasure's gone.'
Bluebeard turned to reassure him.
'Do not despair, oh faint of heart.
We'll get it back ... Come, let us start!'

With that, the real action began ... swordfights around the ship, swordfights down among the audience – rival groups of pirates chasing each other all over the place, now on the stage, now on top of the squealing children. The competition was fierce to regain possession of the map and find the treasure.

Eventually, after a particularly vicious sword fight between Granuaile and Long John Silver, during which both sides sustained slash wounds (hurriedly drawn on with thick felt-tip pens as the action moved for a moment behind the wings), the pirates realised they were all too strong, and the only sensible thing to do was to join forces. They would find the treasure together, then divide it out.

But, on the way back from Treasure Island, Captain Hook tried to double-cross them all, and run off with the treasure for himself, leaving the rest with nothing.

In the very last scene, Captain Hook and Long John Silver battled it out in a fight to the death along the plank. With swords and knives and crutches and hooks, it was a suitably horrible fight, accompanied by much screaming and swearing. It was made even more exciting by the expectation that, at any minute, the fighting pirates would fall off the plank into the audience.

At the end, Long John Silver threw away his sword, and drew a huge dagger from his belt. Raising his arm high in the air, he plunged it straight down into Captain Hook with all his strength.

Jonathan dropped his own sword and clutched at his chest, where a huge red stain suddenly appeared on his white shirt. The red ran down his hands and soaked his shirt sleeves as he staggered around, dripping blood all over the plank.

The children were mesmerised, but nobody noticed that Joan, sitting at the back, had turned chalky white. She stood up, her mouth moving soundlessly as she tried to call out Jonathan's name.

Jonathan did his final death stagger along the plank, moaning pitifully, as the blood poured down his front. Then he performed a spectacular pirouette on the very end of the plank, before falling to the ground, where he lay quite still, blood spreading out in a scarlet pool around him ...

Joan screamed, and screamed, and screamed.

The children panicked, and started screaming too, and some of them ran for the exit. The panic turned into a stampede as all the children tried to get out the small door at the same time, pushing and shoving and screaming even louder as they jammed, and couldn't get out fast enough.

Orla realised what was happening and ran down from the stage to reassure the children, shouting at Felicity to help her.

This panicked the children even more, as they saw the fierce wild figure of Granuaile bearing down on them, with Bluebeard close behind. They became utterly hysterical.

By the time they squeezed out into the laneway in twos and threes, they were wailing and screaming and crying, and the noise was appalling.

Joan's granny had been hanging the washing on the line. She dropped her pegs and came running out to see what was wrong. With a white sheet draped over her front, and flapping behind her, she looked like some kind of mad ghost.

Mr Finnerty was in his garden watering vegetables when he heard the rumpus. Being somehow under the impression that the garage was on fire, he ran down the lane with the hose

trailing after him, and trained it on the garage door. Soon the children were not only hysterical, but thoroughly soaked as well, and the screams could be heard halfway to the village ....

Chapter 24
The Verdict

The concert was a huge success.

Joan was relieved to find out that all the blood came from a plastic bag full of red ink which Jonathan had hidden under his shirt.

The children, once they were home and dry, decided they hadn't had such a marvellous fright in ages. Parents, hearing it was an audience participation play, thought they had walked the plank and fallen into the sea.

All the children wanted to come again the next day, and the gang let them in for free, to make up for the soaking.

On Sunday, to everybody's amazement, Mr and Mrs Finnerty turned up too. Mrs Finnerty spent the entire concert crying her eyes out.

'She was just remembering when her own children were small,' Felicity's mother said afterwards.

The adults paid their 30ps without a murmur, and Mackey's Dad even put in a whole pound.

All the cash was handed over to Felicity.

She was slightly embarrassed, and wanted to share it out with the others. Muggins's face brightened at the idea, but Mackey said no. (He was in a generous mood – his Dad had given him £5.00 for himself.)

'We can't,' he said. 'It's illegal. If you run a benefit for someone, you can't just keep the money for yourselves.'

So that was that! Felicity got to keep the lot.

Chapter 25
Unfinished Business

On Monday morning, they were all sitting around the Captain's Table, still in a state of high excitement about the concert.

'Did you see their faces when I frightened them in the beginning?' Jonathan put on his best pirate voice. 'I – will – split – you – ear – to – ear!'

'You terrified that poor kid with your hook,' Orla said.

'Pirates are meant to be terrifying.'

'Remember when Felicity nearly lost her beard?'

They all laughed. Felicity had got in the way of the big fight between Long John Silver and Granuaile, and her beard had been skewered through by a sword. Muggins had come to the rescue by clamping her hat on her head so that the whole thing couldn't be dragged off.

'Lucky it wasn't a real sword or I'd have no chin left!'

'Harold's violin was really good, wasn't it?' Jonathan sounded surprised.

'Yeah,' Mackey conceded. 'I hope he doesn't come bothering us today.'

'Harold's all right.'

'In small doses.'

Muggins sniggered. 'Did you see Mrs Finnerty? She never stopped bawling!'

'And Mackey's Dad never stopped laughing.'

'He thought it was terrific,' said Mackey proudly. 'Kept saying what a great bunch of kids we were. He was really pleased ... stayed for tea and all ... and he's going to come out every weekend from now on. He thinks it's brilliant out here. I showed him the Red Belly and all the other trees ...' Mackey paused for breath, then continued – 'He said he was sorry about that day in the pub ... He didn't mean to shout and roar at me like that. It was just ... when he saw the cigarette butts ... on account of all the terrible diseases and things you can pick up from public places ...'

Mackey was so engrossed in what he was saying that he didn't notice the odd looks which suddenly appeared on the faces around him.

'Mackey,' Jonathan broke in at last. 'Those butts you gave us – where did you get them?'

Mackey stopped, confused. 'From the pub, of course. Where did you think I got them?'

'I thought they were your Mum's.'

'So did I,' said Muggins, looking slightly sick.

There was an uncomfortable silence, then Joan started to spit, and spit, and spit, wiping her mouth frantically with her sleeve.

Mackey laughed.

Joan stood up furiously, and screamed at Mackey.

'You horrible, horrible boy! You try to kill Jonathan, not once, but twice – now you try to kill the rest of us with your filthy butts. I wish you'd never come here.'

She burst into tears, then turned and ran away through the woods.

Felicity cradled her head in her hands and groaned. 'Not again.'

'Someone will have to fetch her back,' said Orla decisively. 'Jonathan, will you go and talk to her?'

'Me?' asked Jonathan in surprise.

'Yes. She'll listen to you.'

'She will? Why me?'

'Because she thinks everything you say is right.'

'She does?' Jonathan looked astonished.

'Please, Jonathan.'

'OK.' Jonathan shrugged, then got up and went after Joan.

The others sat waiting.

'She hates me, doesn't she?' said Mackey sadly.

'No she doesn't,' Orla reassured him, 'not really. She just thinks Jonathan pays you too much attention.'

'But why should she mind Jonathan paying attention to me?'

'Because she's soft on him, that's why.'

'But I'm not even a girl!' Mackey was totally bewildered.

Felicity giggled, and Orla turned her eyes up to heaven in exasperation.

'Jonathan thinks the sun shines out of your eyes,' explained Felicity. 'He never shuts up about you ... what a great climber you are, what great ideas you have ... He used to talk a lot to Joan, but he's hardly looked at her since you arrived.'

Mackey was still confused.

'OK then, I'll tell Jonathan to stop paying me so much attention.'

'You can't do that!' Felicity was appalled.

'Promise you won't say a word to either of them about this ... promise,' insisted Orla.

'OK, OK, I promise,' Mackey said, not understanding at all.

Jonathan came back at last with Joan in tow. She had an oddly satisfied look on her face.

Jonathan sat down, and Joan sat beside him.

'Right,' said Jonathan, all business. 'We have to discuss this cigarette butt thing.'

'What about it?' Mackey asked warily.

'I have a cold sore in my mouth.' Muggins was gingerly probing about with his finger. 'Maybe my whole mouth will rot away.'

Nobody laughed.

'What diseases exactly can you get from dirty cigarette butts?' Orla voiced the question that was worrying them all.

'How should I know?'

'Didn't you ask your Dad?'

'No, I didn't.'

'Why not?'

'Well,' said Mackey defensively, 'if my Da thought there was any danger he would have had me checked out – now wouldn't he?'

'He probably thought you hadn't smoked any of the butts yet,' Jonathan pointed out.

Mackey was silent.

'Maybe it's one of those awful diseases that don't show up for years.' Felicity looked alarmed.

'Couldn't you ask your Dad?' suggested Orla.

'No jolly fear! He's only just talking to me again. I'm not going to bring up the subject of butts, and have him roaring and shouting and walking out – he mightn't come back this time.'

The gang considered this. He had a point.

'Anyone else?' asked Orla. 'Joan? Couldn't you ask your Granny?'

'No. Why should I? I didn't start this thing.'

'Felicity, would you ask your Mum or Dad?'

Felicity shook her head vehemently. 'I'd have to admit I was smoking butts from the pub, and I've been in enough trouble as it is. Why don't *you* ask your Mum?'

'I wouldn't want to worry her,' Orla admitted, after a pause.

'I never remember having such a big cold sore in my mouth before.' Muggins was still probing anxiously.

'Oh shut up Muggins,' said Jonathan. In truth, he was making the rest of them anxious too.

'We could ask a doctor.'

'But we'd have to pay him.'

' ... and get the money from our folks, so they'd find out anyway.'

'We could ask the teacher if it was school-time,' said Muggins mournfully.

'Well, it's not.' Orla poked him with her elbow. 'Stop making useless suggestions.'

Felicity had been thinking hard. 'Look, there are lots of health magazines down at the newsagents – couldn't we look through them? We might find something.'

'Or the library,' broke in Orla. 'They always know things for school projects.'

'OK. Shops first, library afterwards.'

'And I can get something in the chemist for my cold sore,' said Muggins pathetically.

'Oh, shut up, Muggins! You'd think you were dying.'

'Maybe I am.' Muggins glared resentfully at them. 'And then you'll all be sorry.'

CHAPTER 26
FINDING OUT

It was a fairly sober gang that made their way to the shops after lunch. Muggins's complaints were beginning to sink in, and Jonathan swore he had a peculiar taste in his mouth all of a sudden.

They reached the newsagents, and stood outside arguing about who was to go in.

'We can't all go in, we'd be thrown out.'

'Let the girls go – shops hate boys standing around.'

So Felicity, Orla and Joan went in, and over to the magazine stand.

' "Health and Fitness" ' whispered Orla. 'I'll look at this one.'

' "Healthy Living" ..."Health Facts" ..."Your Health" .... There's loads of stuff here.' Felicity was examining the covers of the magazines.

The took a magazine each, and leafed through them, searching the pages carefully.

'Can I help you ladies?' The assistant, a young man, was smiling pleasantly at them.

'No thank you, we're just looking,' Orla replied.

'Well,' said the young man, still smiling pleasantly, 'if you want to read the magazines, you have to pay for them.'

The girls returned the magazines to the rack, embarrassed.

'Sorry,' mumbled Orla, her face very red. 'We forgot our money ... we'll have to come back.'

The three of them beat a hasty retreat from the shop, feeling like thieves.

'They're fierce mean, they are,' said Mackey darkly. 'They do the same whenever I try to get a read of a comic.'

'We'd better go to the library. At least we can't be told to pay for things there.'

They made their way to the public library, which was at the other end of the village.

'Two people only – that's enough,' suggested Orla.

Jonathan started to climb the steps. 'I'll do it this time,' he said.

'One of the girls should go with you,' warned Mackey. 'People are suspicious of boys.'

'So who else?'

'I'll go,' offered Muggins, who hadn't really been listening, as he was trying to count how many cold sores had appeared since lunchtime.

'You're a girl?'

'What?'

'Joan will go,' said Orla, laughing at her brother, who looked thoroughly confused.

So Joan and Jonathan went in.

The library was cool and quiet, and a woman librarian was working on her own behind the counter.

'May I help you?' she asked with a smile, as they hovered anxiously around, trying to spot suitable leaflets on the counter.

'Yes please,' said Joan. 'We'd like information on smoking.'

'Dirty habit,' advised the librarian. 'I hope you children haven't started already? ... Never, never start .... Cigarettes are dangerous, addictive drugs .... Go right through your body .... Take all the oxygen out of your blood .... Turn your lungs to tar .... Make your teeth yellow and your breath and hair smell like an ashtray ... and poison everyone else too, who has to breathe in your foul smoke .... Filthy habit.'

'We mean,' explained Jonathan, 'do you have any leaflets, please?'

'Sure. Loads of them.' She leaned forward. 'Here. Take some for your friends, your parents, your grannies, your grandads, your uncles, your aunties ....'

'I think we've got enough, thank you,' said Joan, as the woman continued to shove wads of leaflets at them.

Outside, they sat on the steps and shared out the information.

'They're mostly all the same,' declared Felicity, disappointed.

'There's nothing here about butts.' Jonathan was leafing frantically through the pile.

'Nothing here either.'

'They're all just about smoking in general.'

'Go back and ask her,' Orla urged Joan. 'Ask her about butts.'

Joan got up and went back into the library.

The librarian smiled at her again.

'Please, do you have anything on butts?'

'Butts?'

'Yes, diseases you can get from dirty butts?'

'You mean picked up from the ground?' The librarian looked horrified.

'Something like that.'

'You'd better check it out with your doctor. Butts are filthy things ... full of germs.' She shuddered at the thought.

'Thank you,' said Joan dispiritedly, and went outside again to the others.

'Well?'

'What did she say?'

'She said to ask our doctor – that butts are filthy things, and full of germs.'

The gang sat and considered this piece of news in glum silence. They didn't know where to turn next.

'What a lot of long faces!'

They looked up. Joan's granny Dorcas was standing in front of them, dressed in a white track suit, and carrying a sports bag.

'What's the matter?'

Felicity nudged Joan. 'Tell her.'

Joan elbowed Felicity back, annoyed, but said nothing.

Dorcas put down her bag, and motioned the girls to move apart so that she could sit in between them.

'Right, young lady,' she said, addressing Felicity. 'Let's have it.'

Felicity struggled to find the right way to explain. 'Dirty butts ... cigarette butts ... taken from a pub ashtray ... what awful diseases could we get if we smoked them?'

'How often?'

'Only once. Ages ago. When Mackey came first.'

'Well, you all look fine to me.'

'I have terrible cold sores,' moaned Muggins.

'Let me have a look.'

Muggins came over and let Dorcas inspect his mouth.

'I only see one.'

'Well, it's a big one. Did the cigarette do that?'

'Maybe,' Dorcas said slowly, 'and maybe not. You've had cold sores before?'

Muggins admitted that he had.

'Well who knows then?' Dorcas looked at their solemn faces and laughed. 'Cheer up. You're not dead yet.'

'Don't say that, Granny,' admonished Joan crossly. 'It's not funny.'

Dorcas stopped laughing when she realised how anxious they really were. 'There's nothing to worry about,' she reassured them quickly. 'It's not the most hygienic thing to be doing – but then, you don't need me to tell you that, do you?'

They shook their heads, embarrassed.

'However, I think the worst you're likely to get is a bout of allergic blisters on your lips – but since it was ages ago, I think the danger is well and truly past.' She glanced at her watch. 'Heavens, I'm late for my aerobics. Better fly!'

She stood up, slinging the sports-bag over one shoulder, then set off down the village at a jog, in the direction of the local hall.

☆☆☆

Muggins was probing at his mouth again with one finger. 'Hey, guess what? My cold sore feels better already. In fact, I think it's nearly gone.'

172

'Oh, trust him!' said Mackey in exasperation, giving Muggins a shove. 'Now he tells us – after nearly causing a state of emergency!'

They were in a great humour on the way home. The business of the cigarette butts had genuinely frightened them, but now they could laugh at their own fears, since there was no danger any more.

'Don't you ever collect dirty butts again, Ignatius McCarthy,' admonished Jonathan in a stern voice.

'I won't! I won't! Promise. Cross my heart and hope to die. I'm a reformed creature.' Mackey grinned. Now that he was rid of the burden of guilt, his mind was free to think up new mischief.

Orla did a pirouette along the pavement ahead of them.

Mackey shouted after her.

'Hey, Orla! You forgot to drop the veils at the concert!'

Orla stopped. 'What?'

'The Dance of the Seven Veils – you're meant to drop them off one by one till you've got nothing on.'

'But I was wearing a leotard.'

'You're not meant to wear that either.'

Orla looked puzzled. 'What are you talking about?'

Mackey grinned wickedly. 'The Dance of the Seven Veils is a strip-dance. You take off all the veils and dance naked.'

'I don't believe you,' said Orla, going very red.

'It's true.'

'How would you know?'

'A fella told me.'

'What fellow?'

'Fella in the pub. He travelled a lot – saw the dance himself in the Far East and told me all about it. That's why I was laughing when you said you were going to do it for the concert. I just couldn't wait!'

'But nobody here would know about that.'

'Course they would. It's a world-famous dance.'

'I don't believe you,' Orla said for the second time, doubt creeping into her voice.

'It's true. Ask anyone you like,' Mackey laughed.

'Don't mind him,' advised Joan. 'He's only trying to cause trouble as usual.'

☆☆☆

But as soon as she got home, Orla went seeking her mother.

Her father was in the kitchen, apron on, cooking a big family fry-up.

'Where's Mum?'

'Gone for a walk with the little ones. What's wrong?'

'Dad, did you know the Dance of the Seven Veils is a strip-dance?'

'Well ... yes ... the original one, at least.' Mr Duggan looked at his daughter in surprise. It was rare to see Orla so upset.

'I never knew! Why didn't you stop me?'

Mr Duggan laughed. 'Orla, my love, I didn't think for one minute that you were going to take off your clothes – and it's a lovely name for a dance anyway.'

'But I didn't know what it really was! ... Oh, I've made such a fool of myself.'

Orla was in tears now, and her father tried to comfort her with a hug. 'There are very few people in this life who don't make a fool of themselves at some time or other,' he said gently. 'Besides, who cares?'

'I care,' sobbed Orla.

And indeed, it was weeks before she could remember the concert without her face burning with shame at the thought.

Chapter 27
Up The Red Belly

Felicity slipped out early one morning, just before breakfast.

It was time.

She wanted the woods to herself, before anyone else was stirring. Today, Felicity was going to climb the Red Belly.

Last night she had managed to touch a bit of pattern on her bedroom wallpaper that had always been out of reach. She had grown this summer, and that was the proof.

The woods were quiet, with the clean sharp smell of a summer morning. In the clearing, sunlight speckled down on the brown loam which formed the woodland floor. The Red Belly was waiting. She could almost hear it calling ... and she knew, without a doubt, that today the Red Belly would be hers.

She hadn't tried to climb it in a while – not since the day of the accident with Harold's glasses.

Now she was ready.

She negotiated the first couple of footholds easily, then found the deep fingerhold that she remembered from before. This time, instead of getting stuck, she discovered another handhold to the far left, and slightly higher up. She couldn't understand why she hadn't found it sooner.

Hauling herself upwards, she slipped, and clutched at the bark for dear life until she found her foothold again. She knew she ought to be moving faster. Jonathan always said you had to take the Red Belly at a run. Mackey had done just that the first time. But it was harder than it looked.

She reached around the trunk of the tree until she located further holds, small and precarious. Slowly she worked her way upwards.

The first branch was nearly overhead now, and she would have to release her handholds to try for it. But today she would not fall. Today, she could even fly.

Sizing up the distance carefully, she pushed with her toes, and grabbed upwards for the branch. Her hands locked around it safely. Swinging free for a moment, she quickly walked her feet up the trunk until she got a leg over the branch too. Suddenly she was astride it, and looking down at the long drop to the ground.

At last!

She sat there for a while, just savouring her victory. Then she continued on up the tree, finding little difficulty with the rest, right up to the Crow's Nest. She settled into the hollow between the branches, where she had wanted to be for so long.

She found all the hidey-holes. Here was Mackey's wrestling magazine, wrapped in a plastic bag ... the logbook ... a pencil ... survival rations (seeds and raisins) ... Dara's letters. She sat in the Crow's Nest for ages, just getting the feel of it. Then she began to examine the branches overhead, figuring out the best route from here. She chose the most direct one, straight upwards.

The branch was thick at first, but thinned out gradually as she climbed, until she could feel it sway a bit. Up, up she climbed, until she was clear above the level of the woods, and could see for miles in every direction.

There was the main road that led to the fields where they'd had their picnic; and the church spire, matching her for height. In the other direction was the sea, barely visible on the horizon; and the smoky haze of the city itself.

She turned slowly and carefully, until she faced in the direction of Conker Road. She could see right up the lane and into all the gardens.

There was Joan's house – and Joan herself, having breakfast at the table by the dining-room window. Felicity swayed on her perch, willing her friend to look up. Joan kept on eating. Felicity tried to peer down to the ground below, but all she could see were treetops. She had never been so high before.

She looked up at the houses again. Joan was standing at her back door, waving in the direction of the Red Belly. She had spotted her. Felicity cradled the branch against her chest, then cupped her hands to shout: 'Jooo-aaan!'

The answer came back surprisingly clear, 'Fel-iiii-citeeee?'

'It's meeeeee!'

Joan gave a loud whoop, and ran down the garden yelling, 'Jonathan! Jonathan! Felicity's up the Red Belly!' She ran to Felicity's house and banged on the back door. Jonathan opened it, and the two of them stood staring at the Red Belly.

Then, with a wave, they disappeared out in the direction of the front road.

In no time at all, the whole gang was tearing down the lane, shouting at her as they ran. Felicity could hear them clumping through the woods, and she climbed back down to the Crow's Nest. When she looked over the edge, they were all there, below her.

'Hold on! We're coming up!'

Jonathan was the first to reach her, then Joan, followed by Orla, Mackey and Muggins. Four of them managed to squeeze into the Crow's Nest, and Mackey and Muggins sat on a branch beside them.

'Great,' said Jonathan with satisfaction. 'Now we can hold all our meetings up here.'

'But we'll have to give the Captain's Table to Harold,' wailed Joan.

The others looked at her in dismay. They had almost forgotten about the deal with Harold. They'd never thought things would happen so fast.

'We shouldn't have promised.'

'Well, we can't keep the whole woods to ourselves forever,' said Orla with a sigh. 'If it wasn't Harold, it would be somebody else – the little ones on the road are growing up fast. They'll all be allowed out into the woods in a year or two.'

'That's true,' agreed Felicity sadly. 'It won't be the same then, will it?'

Orla shrugged. 'Maybe we'll be too old to want to bother with the Red Belly.'

'No way!' Muggins looked distraught, and the rest of them shook their heads.

'I'll never be too old for the Red Belly,' declared Felicity with conviction, 'and if growing up means not climbing trees any more, then I don't want to grow up ever.'

'Me neither,' said Mackey.

'Oh, who cares about growing up?' Jonathan broke in impatiently. 'The Red Belly is still ours, and we're having our very first meeting in the Crow's Nest. I vote we put it in the logbook and all sign to make it official.' He produced the logbook and pencil, and turned to a brand new page.

'I must write to Dara – won't he be surprised!' exclaimed Felicity happily as everyone signed their names.

'This is the second bit of good news I've had this morning already,' announced Joan, looking suddenly mysterious.

'And what's the other bit?' asked Felicity.

'My Mum's expecting a baby!'

'Oh, Joan! That's great.' Felicity gave her a big hug.

'That'll be a change for you,' Orla laughed. 'You'll have loads of minding to do, wait and see.'

'Babies do nothing but cry,' warned Mackey. 'You won't get any sleep. I stayed with my auntie last year and I was glad to get home again – she had a right screamer.'

'I don't mind,' said Joan, quite unconcerned. 'It's not due for ages yet anyway.'

'I haven't had my breakfast,' Muggins suddenly remembered, as his tummy rumbled.

'And I didn't finish mine.' Jonathan was feeling hungry too.

'I'm going down to tell my Mum,' declared Felicity, restless with excitement.

'Let's go!'

So they climbed back down the Red Belly, letting Felicity come last, as she wanted the Crow's Nest to herself again just for a minute or two.

The others were all waiting on the ground by the time Felicity reached the last branch. Then a terrible thing happened ...

She got stuck.

Suddenly the ground seemed miles away. The void below rose to swallow her up every time she tried to move. The trees swirled in sickening waves around her. She sat on the branch, eyes tightly closed, unable to manage the about-turn necessary for the last bit of the descent.

'Jump,' shouted Jonathan.

'I'll break something.'

'Hang from the branch by your fingers and just drop.'

'It's too far.'

'Do you want us to get a ladder?'

'Don't you dare,' yelled Felicity, outraged into opening her eyes. 'I'll be down in a minute – just stop watching me!'

The gang sat on the ground to wait for her.

Ten minutes later, Felicity was still pondering the problem, and the gang had run out of suggestions.

Mackey got fed up and wandered off to explore.

Felicity knew she'd have to make an effort – she couldn't sit there all day.

'I think I'm ready now,' she called, taking a deep breath.

But before she could move, Mackey reappeared.

'Look what I found,' he shouted.

In his hands he held a round object, like a small crinkly brown football.

'Watch it,' warned Jonathan. 'That's a nest.'

'It's OK,' said Mackey. 'It's dead – look,' and he shook it vigorously. Then he grinned, full of mischief. 'Here, catch!'

He threw the brown thing towards Jonathan. The gang scattered as it landed with a thump beneath the Red Belly. It broke open, and a swarm of wasps rose in a black cloud, enveloping Felicity on the branch above. She screamed, and fell out of the tree.

Suddenly there were wasps everywhere: on faces and necks and arms and legs, tangled in hair and clothes, stinging ... stinging ... stinging ...

The gang fled in panic, howling with pain and fright.

Out of the woods they raced, and up the lane to the front road, desperate to escape the trail of angry wasps streaming after them ....

Chapter 28
Where Is Felicity?

Jonathan sat on a kitchen chair, squirming, as his mother anointed his stings with iodine. It was all she could find; the tubes of antihistamine and antiseptic had somehow gone missing from the first-aid box.

She had done his face already, and his arms and legs, also his head – for he had come home with wasps in his hair, and had been stung there as well.

He looked appalling – covered with swollen bumps and red polka-dots of iodine, his blond hair streaked scarlet like some mad punk-rocker's.

'Keep still,' said Mrs Kelly. 'I'm nearly finished.'

There was a knock on the back door.

'Come in.'

It was Joan. She was covered with stings too, but her granny had used a colourless ointment on them. She grinned when she saw Jonathan.

'Hi Mrs Kelly.'

'Hello Joan.'

'Hi Jonathan.'

Jonathan grunted, and Joan started to giggle.

'What are you sniggering at?'

'Sorry ... but you look so funny!'

'You're not so hot yourself,' Jonathan said crossly.

Joan tried to change the subject.

'How's Felicity?'

There was a deathly silence.

Mrs Kelly looked at her in surprise, iodine bottle arrested in mid-air.

'What do you mean, "How's Felicity"?'

Joan looked confused. 'I mean, where is she? Is she all right?'

'I thought she was with you,' said Jonathan in a small voice.

'No, I haven't seen her.'

They stared at each other, horrified, remembering only too well the last time they had seen her.

The nest under the tree ...

The wasps ...

Felicity falling ...

'Oh my God,' whispered Jonathan.

He jumped up and ran for the door, overturning the kitchen chair in his haste. Joan, with a guilty glance at Mrs Kelly, bolted after him.

'What's wrong? What's wrong?' cried Mrs Kelly. But they were gone.

She quickly corked the iodine, and without even stopping to remove her apron, ran after them.

Down the lane they raced, fear spurring them on; into the woods, and right through to the clearing.

The ground was littered with gooseberries, which popped beneath their feet.

And Felicity was still there.

She lay on the ground by the Red Belly, unconscious, one arm stuck out at a very odd angle.

Beside her was Harold, sitting firmly on an upturned bucket; and from underneath him came the rasp of angry wasps, as they beat against the walls of their plastic prison.

CHAPTER 29
ALL'S WELL

The gang was visiting Felicity in hospital; Harold was there too, as Mrs Kelly insisted that Jonathan should bring him along.

They all looked as if they ought to be in hospital too, being covered in red lumps – except Harold, of course. Jonathan's condition, in fact, had caused much confusion when they came in the front door, as a misguided porter tried to rush him down to casualty.

Now they were sprawled out over Felicity's bed, guzzling grapes and sweets that relatives and neighbours had sent in.

'Get off my foot, you lot,' ordered Felicity. 'I'm supposed to be minding it.'

'Sorry.' They moved up the bed a bit.

Felicity was looking quite well – considering.

She had a broken right arm, now securely plastered, and a horridly bruised and swollen right ankle, which was only badly sprained. She was covered with stings too, and one eye was completely closed up. They were keeping her in hospital for a while until she could walk on her ankle, as she couldn't manage a crutch with the broken arm.

The gang were in a talkative mood. They hadn't felt much like talking yesterday, after Felicity was

187

taken away by ambulance. Those first terrible hours, until news came through from the hospital, were engraved on all their minds.

The truth was that each of them felt guilty.

They had all seen Felicity falling out of the tree, but were so intent on escaping from the wasps and having their stings attended to, that none of them had given her another thought.

Except Harold.

'It's lucky I came along,' he announced proudly. 'I saved Felicity from being stung to death.'

'Maybe you did, too,' agreed Felicity. 'If I had woken up, the wasps would have attacked again.'

'So now you're quits,' Mackey pointed out.

'What?'

'You saved Harold from drowning, he saved you from the wasps.'

'Oh, I see.' Felicity laughed. 'Well, that's fair enough.'

'What I want to know,' said Jonathan, turning to Harold, 'is how you got the wasps into the bucket?'

They had all been wondering about that.

'I just put the bucket over them,' Harold explained. 'They were crawling on top of the nest in a heap – trying to get back in, I suppose.'

'And how come you just happened to have a bucket with you in the first place?'

'For the gooseberries. I was bringing them home.'

Mackey gave a hoot of laughter. 'You pinched them from Old Fitzy's garden!'

'I did not,' said Harold indignantly. 'He gave them to me.'

'You're joking!'

'He never did!'

'He wouldn't!'

'He did so. I asked him.'

'You *asked* him?' The gang were totally flabbergasted now.

'Yes.' Harold was pleased to be the centre of attention. 'I was exploring in the woods, and I climbed Mr Fitzhenry's wall and saw the gooseberries ... and he was there too ... so I asked him could I have some ... and he said yes, that they were nearly finished and would only go to waste anyway ... he even gave me the bucket to put them in.'

There was a long silence, as the gang stared at Harold with new respect.

☆☆☆

Felicity came home the week before school began again.

As it was the end of the summer, her accident was not quite the disaster it would have been had it happened earlier. When she went back to school she couldn't do any written homework for weeks. Even after her plaster was taken off, she had to do exercises to make her muscles strong enough to hold a pen again. And best of all – she couldn't do any housework.

Jonathan had to do the lot.

He even had to make Felicity's bed every day. 'It's the least you can do,' his mother insisted firmly. She still found it hard to understand how Jonathan could have forgotten about Felicity the way he had.

Jonathan complained bitterly, he hated it all so much.

'Now you know how I felt,' said Felicity.

Everyone wanted to write things on Felicity's plaster cast.

Muggins drew funny cartoon faces.

Joan signed her name with a flourish.

Orla painted a pink ballerina on the elbow.

Jonathan, with more grace than he had shown in a long time, wrote:

'Daily chores

Are terrible bores

I'll do mine

If you'll do yours.'

Then he spat on the plaster and pressed in his thumb print, to seal the bargain.

And Mackey, having pinched a bottle of red nail polish from his mother's dressing-table, wrote in big capital letters, running the full length of the plaster:

'UP THE RED BELLY!'

Other Titles From Wolfhound Press

Skyscraper Ted and Other Zany Verse
Margot Bosonnet

Introduce kids to crazy, wacky verse – and fun.
From children learning the first fun words and their
slithery sounds, to young readers tackling one page at
a time, Skyscraper Ted is a breath of fresh air!

ISBN 0 86327 406 4

The Silver Chalice
Shelagh Jones

A local museum visit for eleven-year-old Paul
Sheehan is the beginning of a time travel trip of a
lifetime, but exactly whose life time is not so clear.
Involving distraught monks, modern day biker
Vikings, a stubborn pig called Tantony and a lost
chalice at the heart of the search, Paul tries to
unravel a mess that's over one thousand years old!
For readers of eight up.

ISBN 0 86327 540 0